William Shakespeare

Shakespeare's Comedy of Love's Labour's Lost

William Shakespeare

Shakespeare's Comedy of Love's Labour's Lost

ISBN/EAN: 9783744788526

Printed in Europe, USA, Canada, Australia, Japan

Cover: Foto ©Andreas Hilbeck / pixelio.de

More available books at **www.hansebooks.com**

PIC DU MIDI D' OSSAU, NAVARRE,

SHAKESPEARE'S

COMEDY OF

LOVE'S LABOUR 'S LOST.

EDITED, WITH NOTES,

BY

WILLIAM J. ROLFE, A.M.,

FORMERLY HEAD MASTER OF THE HIGH SCHOOL, CAMBRIDGE, MASS.

WITH ENGRAVINGS.

NEW YORK:

HARPER & BROTHERS, PUBLISHERS,

FRANKLIN SQUARE.

1881.

ENGLISH CLASSICS.

Edited by WM. J. ROLFE, A.M.

Illustrated.   16mo, Cloth, 56 cents per volume ; Paper, 40 cents per volume.

SHAKESPEARE'S WORKS.

The Merchant of Venice.	The Taming of the Shrew.
Othello.	All 's Well that Ends Well.
Julius Cæsar.	Coriolanus.
A Midsummer-Night's Dream.	The Comedy of Errors.
Macbeth.	Cymbeline.
Hamlet.	Antony and Cleopatra.
Much Ado about Nothing.	Measure for Measure.
Romeo and Juliet.	Merry Wives of Windsor.
As You Like It.	Love's Labour 's Lost.
The Tempest.	Two Gentlemen of Verona.
Twelfth Night.	Timon of Athens.
The Winter's Tale.	Troilus and Cressida.
King John.	Henry VI. Part I.
Richard II.	Henry VI. Part II.
Henry IV. Part I.	Henry VI. Part III.
Henry IV. Part II.	Pericles, Prince of Tyre.
Henry V.	The Two Noble Kinsmen.
Richard III.	Venus and Adonis, Lucrece, etc.
Henry VIII.	Sonnets.
King Lear.	Titus Andronicus.

GOLDSMITH'S SELECT POEMS.
GRAY'S SELECT POEMS.

Published by HARPER & BROTHERS, New York.

☞ *Any of the above works will be sent by mail, postage prepaid, to any part of the United States, on receipt of the price.*

CONTENTS.

A VIEW IN NAVARRE.

SPANISH GENTLEMAN AND FRENCH LADY OF 16TH CENTURY.

INTRODUCTION

TO

LOVE'S LABOUR 'S LOST.

I. THE HISTORY OF THE PLAY.

THE earliest edition of *Love's Labour 's Lost* (or *Love's La-bours Lost*, as Mr. Furnivall believes we should write it) that has come down to us is a quarto published in 1598, with the following title-page (as given in the Camb. ed.):

A | Pleasant | Conceited Comedie | called, | Loues labors lost. | As it was presented before her Highnes | this last Christmas. | Newly corrected and augmented | *By W. Shake-*

spere. | Imprinted at London by *W. W.* | for *Cutbert Burby.* | 1598.

No entry of the play upon the Stationers' Registers appears before January 22, 1606–7, when it was transferred by Burby to N. Ling, who may have brought out a new edition, though no copy of it or reference to it is now known. A second quarto, published in 1631, "by W. S. for *Iohn Smethwicke*" (to whom Ling assigned the copyright in 1607) is apparently reprinted from the folio of 1623.

The earliest mention of the play that has been discovered is in the following lines from a poem entitled *Alba, or the Months Mind of a Melancholy Lover,* by " R. T. Gentleman " (Robert Tofte), published by Burby in 1598:

> " Love's Labour Lost I once did see, a Play
> Y-cleped so, so called to my paine.
> Which I to heare to my small Ioy did stay,
> Giving attendance on my froward Dame :
>   My misgiving minde presaging to me ill,
>   Yet was I drawne to see it 'gainst my will,
>
> *   *   *   *   *   *   *
>
> Each Actor plaid in cunning wise his part,
> But chiefly Those entrapt in Cupids snare ;
> Yet All was fained, 't was not from the hart,
> They seemde to grieve, but yet they felt no care :
>   'T was I that Griefe (indeed) did beare in brest,
>   The others did but make a show in Iest."

It is included in Meres's list, printed in the same year (see *M. N. D.* p. 9, or *C. of E.* p. 102).*

The quarto of 1598 professes to be " newly corrected and augmented," and there can be little doubt that it is the revised form of a play written some years before, and not improbably Shakespeare's first play. Drake, Delius, and Fleay date it in 1591, Stoke in 1591–2, Chalmers in 1592, and

---

* On the play of " *Loue labours wonne,*" which Meres associates with it, see *A. IV.* p. 9 fol.

Malone in 1594. Furnivall is inclined to make the date 1588-9,* and White "probably not later than 1588."

Among the marks of an early style (cf. Stokes, *Chron. Order of Shakespeare's Plays*, p. 28) may be mentioned : the introduction of well - known old characters (besides "the Nine Worthies," we have what Biron, in v. 2. 540, calls "the pedant, the braggart, the hedge priest, the fool, and the boy "†); the observance of the "unities;" the abundance of rhyme, the doggerel, the sonnets‡ (occasionally as speeches); the alliteration, or "affecting the letter," as Holofernes calls it; the quibbles, antitheses, repartees, "the sparkles of wit, like a blaze of fireworks" (Schlegel); the proverbial expressions; the peculiar and pedantic grammatical constructions; the words used in their native forms; the display of learning; the pairs of characters; the disguising and changing of persons; the chorus-like, alternate answers; the strained dialogue, etc. It is "a play of conversation and situation" (Furnivall), in which "depth of characterization is subordinate to elegance and sprightliness of dialogue" (Staunton). There is a want of reality about it all; even the occasion—a princess acting as an ambassadress—is unnatural.

The play is poorly printed in both the quarto and the folio, and the repetition of sundry typographical errors proves that the latter was set up from a copy of the former. There are, however, variations in the two texts which indi-

---

* He says : "I have no hesitation in picking out this as Shakspere's earliest play. The reason that has induced some critics to put it later is, I believe, that it is much more carefully worked-at and polished than some of the other early plays." This he ascribes to the revision of the play ; and he refers to some striking evidences of the correction, which will be found in our *Notes* below.

† In the prefixes and stage-directions of the folio, Armado is often "the braggart," Holofernes "the pedant," Nathaniel "the curate," Costard "the clown," and Moth "the boy" or "page."

‡ Some of these sonnets were printed by Jaggard in *The Passionate Pilgrim*, 1599. For others, cf. *Sonn.* 127, 137.

cate that the editors of the folio were occasionally indebted
to some other authority than the quarto.

II. THE SOURCES OF THE PLOT.

The plot, so far as we know, was original with Shakespeare.
Dowden remarks: "The play is precisely such a one as a
clever young man might imagine, who had come lately from
the country — with its 'daisies pied and violets blue,' its
'merry larks,' its maidens who 'bleach their summer smocks,'
its pompous parish schoolmaster, and its dull constable (a
great public official in his own eyes)—to the town, where he
was surrounded by more brilliant unrealities, and affectations
of dress, of manner, of language, and of ideas. *Love's Labour 's Lost* is a dramatic plea on behalf of nature and of
common-sense against all that is unreal and affected." But, as
White says, "that the play is founded upon some older work,
its undramatic character, its needless fulness of detail, its air
of artificial romance, and the attribution of particular personal traits—such as black eyes and a dark complexion to
one, great size to another, and a face pitted with the small-
pox to another of the ladies, and the merely incidental hints
that one of the king's friends is an officer in the army and
extremely youthful—seem unmistakable evidence; and that
the story is of French origin is as clearly shown by the na-
tionality of the titles, the Gallicism of calling a love-letter a
capon, the appearance of the strong French negative *point*
twice, and the use of *seigneur* instead of *signior*." Rev. Jo-
seph Hunter, in his *New Illustrations* (vol. i. p. 256) suggests
that the poet may have got a hint from Monstrelet's *Chron-
icles*, according to which Charles, King of Navarre, surren-
dered to the King of France the castle of Cherbourg, the
county of Evreux, and other lordships for the Duchy of
Nemours and a promise of 200,000 gold crowns. Sundry
passages which appear to have been borrowed or imitated
from other writers will be pointed out in the *Notes*.

III. CRITICAL COMMENTS ON THE PLAY.

[*From Schlegel's " Dramatic Literature."**]

Love's Labour's Lost is numbered among the pieces of his youth. It is a humorsome display of frolic; a whole cornucopia of the most vivacious jokes is emptied into it. Youth is certainly perceivable in the lavish superfluity of labour in the execution: the unbroken succession of plays on words, and sallies of every description, hardly leave the spectator time to breathe; the sparkles of wit fly about in such profusion that they resemble a blaze of fireworks; while the dialogue, for the most part, is in the same hurried style in which the passing masks at a carnival attempt to banter each other. The young king of Navarre, with three of his courtiers, has made a vow to pass three years in rigid retirement, and devote them to the study of wisdom; for that purpose he has banished all female society from his court, and imposed a penalty on the intercourse with women. But scarcely has he, in a pompous harangue, worthy of the most heroic achievements, announced this determination, when the daughter of the King of France appears at his court, in the name of her old and bedridden father, to demand the restitution of a province which he held in pledge. Compelled to give her audience, he falls immediately in love with her. Matters fare no better with his companions, who on their parts renew an old acquaintance with the princess's attendants. Each, in heart, is already false to his vow, without knowing that the wish is shared by his associates; they overhear one another, as they in turn confide their sorrows in a love-ditty to the solitary forest: every one jeers and confounds the one who follows him. Biron, who from the beginning was the most satirical among them, at last steps forth, and rallies the king and the two others, till the discov-

---

* *Lectures on Dramatic Art and Literature,* by A. W. Schlegel; Black's translation, revised by Morrison (London, 1846), p. 383 fol.

ery of a love-letter forces him also to hang down his head.
He extricates himself and his companions from their dilem-
ma by ridiculing the folly of the broken vow, and, after a noble eulogy on women, invites them to swear new allegiance
to the colours of love. This scene is inimitable, and the
crowning beauty of the whole. The manner in which they
afterwards prosecute their love-suits in masks and disguise,
and in which they are tricked and laughed at by the ladies,
who are also masked and disguised, is, perhaps, spun out too
long. It may be thought, too, that the poet, when he suddenly announces the death of the King of France, and makes
the princess postpone her answer to the prince's serious ad-
vances till the expiration of the period of her mourning,
and impose, besides, a heavy penance on him for his levity,
drops the proper comic tone. But the tone of raillery, which
prevails throughout the piece, made it hardly possible to
bring about a more satisfactory conclusion : after such extravagance, the characters could not return to sobriety, except under the presence of some foreign influence. The
grotesque figures of Don Armado, a pompous fantastic
Spaniard, a couple of pedants, and a clown, who between
whiles contribute to the entertainment, are the creation of a
whimsical imagination, and well adapted as foils for the wit
of so vivacious a society.

[*From Coleridge's " Notes and Lectures upon Shakspeare." **]

The characters in this play are either impersonated out
of Shakspeare's own multiformity by imaginative self-posi-
tion, or out of such as a country town and schoolboy's observation might supply — the curate, the schoolmaster, the
Armado, who even in my time was not extinct in the cheap-
er inns of North Wales), and so on. The satire is chiefly
on follies of words. Biron and Rosaline are evidently the
pre-existent state of Benedict and Beatrice, and so, perhaps,

* Coleridge's Works (Harper's edition), vol. iv. p. 79 fol.

is Boyet of Lafeu, and Costard of the Tapster in *Measure for Measure;* and the frequency of the rhymes, the sweetness as well as the smoothness of the metre, and the number of acute and fancifully illustrated aphorisms, are all as they ought to be in a poet's youth. True genius begins by generalizing and condensing; it ends in realizing and expanding. It first collects the seeds.

Yet if this juvenile drama had been the only one extant of our Shakspeare, and we possessed the tradition only of his riper works, or accounts of them in writers who had not even mentioned this play, how many of Shakspeare's characteristic features might we not still have discovered in *Love's Labour 's Lost*, though as in a portrait taken of him in his boyhood !

I can never sufficiently admire the wonderful activity of thought throughout the whole of the first scene of the play, rendered natural, as it is, by the choice of the characters, and the whimsical determination on which the drama is founded. A whimsical determination certainly ; yet not altogether so very improbable to those who are conversant in the history of the Middle Ages, with their Courts of Love, and all that lighter drapery of chivalry, which engaged even mighty kings with a sort of serio-comic interest, and may well be supposed to have occupied more completely the smaller princes, at a time when the noble's or prince's court contained the only theatre of the domain or principality. This sort of story, too, was admirably suited to Shakspeare's times, when the English court was still the foster-mother of the state and the muses ; and when, in consequence, the courtiers, and men of rank and fashion, affected a display of wit, point, and sententious observation that would be deemed intolerable at present, but in which a hundred years of controversy, involving every great political, and every dear domestic, interest, had trained all but the lowest classes to participate. Add to this the very style of the sermons of the time, and the eagerness of the Protestants to distinguish themselves by long and frequent preaching, it will be found that, from the reign of Henry VIII. to the abdication of James II., no country ever received such a national education as England.

Hence the comic matter chosen in the first instance is a ridiculous imitation or apery of this constant striving after logical precision, and subtle opposition of thoughts, together with a making the most of every conception or image, by expressing it under the least expected property belonging to it, and this, again, rendered specially absurd by being applied to the most current subjects and occurrences. The phrases and modes of combination in argument were caught by the most ignorant from the custom of the age, and their ridiculous misapplication of them is most amusingly exhibited in Costard; whilst examples suited only to the gravest propositions and impersonations, or apostrophes to abstract thoughts impersonated, which are in fact the natural language only of the most vehement agitations of the mind, are adopted by the coxcombry of Armado as mere artifices of ornament.

The same kind of intellectual action is exhibited in a more serious and elevated strain in many other parts of this play. Biron's speech at the end of the fourth act is an excellent specimen of it. It is logic clothed in rhetoric; but observe how Shakspeare, in his twofold being of poet and philosopher, avails himself of it to convey profound truths in the most lively images—the whole remaining faithful to the character supposed to utter the lines, and the expressions themselves constituting a further development of that character.

[Here Coleridge quotes the 41 lines from " Other slow arts entirely keep the brain " to the end of the speech.]

This is quite a study: sometimes you see this youthful god of poetry connecting disparate thoughts purely by means of resemblances in the words expressing them — a thing in character in lighter comedy, especially of that kind in which Shakspeare delights, namely, the purposed display of wit, though sometimes, too, disfiguring his graver scenes; but more often you may see him doubling the natural connection or order of logical consequence in the thoughts by the introduction of an artificial and sought-for resemblance in the words, as, for instance, in the third line of the play—

"And then grace us in the disgrace of death;"

this being a figure often having its force and propriety, as justified by the law of passion, which, inducing in the mind an unusual activity, seeks for means to waste its superfluity —when in the highest degree—in lyric repetitions and sublime tautology (*at her feet he bowed, he fell, he lay down; at her feet he bowed, he fell; where he bowed, there he fell down dead*); and, in lower degrees, in making the words themselves the subjects and materials of that surplus action, and for the same cause that agitates our limbs, and forces our very gestures into a tempest in states of high excitement.

The mere style of narration in *Love's Labour's Lost*, like that of Ægeon in the first scene of the *Comedy of Errors*, and of the Captain in the second scene of *Macbeth*, seems imitated with its defects and its beauties from Sir Philip Sidney; whose *Arcadia*, though not then published, was already well known in manuscript copies, and could hardly have escaped the notice and admiration of Shakspeare as the friend and client of the Earl of Southampton. The chief defect consists in the parentheses and parenthetic thoughts and descriptions, suited neither to the passion of the speaker nor the purpose of the person to whom the information is to be given, but manifestly betraying the author himself —not by way of continuous under-song, but—palpably, and so as to show themselves addressed to the general reader. However, it is not unimportant to notice how strong a pre-

B

sumption the diction and allusions of this play afford, that, though Shakspeare's acquirements in the dead languages might not be such as we suppose in a learned education, his habits had, nevertheless, been scholastic, and those of a student. For a young author's first work almost always bespeaks his recent pursuits; and his first observations of life are either drawn from the immediate employments of his youth, and from the characters and images most deeply impressed on his mind in the situations in which those employments had placed him, or else they are fixed on such objects and occurrences in the world as are easily connected with, and seem to bear upon, his studies and the hitherto exclusive subjects of his meditation. Just as Ben Jonson, who applied himself to the drama, after having served in Flanders, fills his earliest plays with true or pretended soldiers—the wrongs and neglects of the former, and the absurd boasts and knavery of their counterfeits. So Lessing's first comedies are placed in the universities, and consist of events and characters conceivable in an academic life.

I will only further remark the sweet and tempered gravity with which Shakspeare in the end draws the only fitting moral which such a drama afforded. Here Rosaline rises up to the full height of Beatrice.

[*From Hazlitt's " Characters of Shakespear's Plays." **]

If we were to part with any of the author's comedies, it should be this. Yet we should be loath to part with Don Adriano de Armado, that mighty potentate of nonsense ; or his page, that handful of wit ; with Nathaniel the curate, or Holofernes the schoolmaster, and their dispute after dinner, on " the golden cadences of poetry ;" with Costard the clown, or Dull the constable. Biron is too accomplished a character to be lost to the world, and yet he could not appear with-

* *Characters of Shakespear's Plays*, by William Hazlitt, edited by W Carew Hazlitt, (London, 1869), p. 206 fol.

out his fellow-courtiers and the King; and if we were to
leave out the ladies, the gentlemen would have no mistresses. So that we believe we must let the whole play
stand as it is, and we shall hardly venture to " set a mark of
reprobation on it." Still we have some objections to the
style, which we think savours more of the pedantic spirit of
Shakespear's time than of his own genius—more of contro-
versial divinity, and the logic of Peter Lombard, than of the
inspiration of the muse. It transports us quite as much to
the manners of the court, and the quirks of courts of law, as
to the scenes of nature, or the fairy-land of his own imagination.

Shakespear has set himself to imitate the tone of polite
conversation then prevailing among the fair, the witty, and
the learned; and he has imitated it but too faithfully. It is
as if the hand of Titian had been employed to give grace to
the curls of a full-bottomed periwig, or Raphael had attempted to give expression to the tapestry figures in the House of
Lords. Shakespear has put an excellent description of this
fashionable jargon into the mouth of the critical Holofernes,
" as too picked, too spruce, too affected, too odd, too peregrinate, as I may call it;" and nothing can be more marked
than the difference when he breaks loose from the trammels
he had imposed on himself, " as light as bird from brake,"
and speaks in his own person.

[From Verplanck's " Shakespeare." *]

There is a general concurrence of opinion, both traditional
and critical, that this play was among Shakespeare's earliest
dramatic works. . . . Its general resemblance of style and
thought to his other early works, and especially the "frequency of the rhymes, the sweetness as well as the smoothness of the metre, and the number of acute and fancifully

* *The Illustrated Shakespeare*, edited by G. C. Verplanck (New York,
1847), vol. ii. p. 5 of *L. L. L.*

illustrated aphorisms," all correspond with the idea of a youthful work; while, as in others of his early works, we also find in the personages the rudiments of characters, slightly sketched, to which he afterwards returned, and, without repeating himself, presented them again, in a varied and more individualized and living form. Thus, Biron contains within him the germs both of Benedick and of Jaques; of the one in his colloquial and mocking mood, and of the other in his graver moralities. Rosaline is (in Coleridge's phrase) "the pre-existent state of Beatrice;" though she is as yet a Beatrice of the imagination, drawn from books or report, rather than one painted from familiar acquaintance.

Both the characters and the dialogue are such as youthful talent might well invent, without much knowledge of real life, and would indeed be likely to invent, before the experience and observation of varied society. The comedy presents a picture, not of the true every-day life of the great or the beautiful, but exhibits groups of such brilliant personages as they might be supposed to appear in the artificial conversation, the elaborate and continual effort to surprise or dazzle by wit or elegance, which was the prevailing taste of the age, in its literature, its poetry, and even its pulpit; and in which the nobles and beauties of the day were accustomed to array themselves for exhibition, as in their state attire, for occasions of display. All this, when the leading idea was once caught, was quite within the reach of the young poet to imitate or surpass, with little or no personal knowledge of aristocratic—or what would now be termed fashionable—society. English literature, a century later, afforded a striking example of the success of a very young author in carrying to its perfection a similar affectation of artificial wit, and studied conversational brilliancy—I mean Congreve, whose comedies, the admiration of their own age, for their fertility of fantastically gay dialogue, bright conceits, and witty repartees, are still read for their abundance of lively imagery and play of language, the " reciprocation of conceits and the clash of wit,"—although the personages of his scene, and all that they do and think, are wholly remote from the truth, the feeling, and the manners of real life. These productions, so remarkable in their way, were written before Congreve's twenty-fifth year ; and his first and most brilliant comedy (*The Old Bachelor*) was acted when he was yet a minor. His talent, thus early ripe, did not afterwards expand or refine itself into the nobler power of teaching "the morals of the heart," nor even into the delightful gift of embodying the passing scenes of real life in graphic and durable pictures. But his writings afford a memorable proof how soon the graces and brilliant effects of mere intellect can be acquired, while those works of genius which require the co-operation and the knowledge of man's moral nature are of slower and later growth.

This comedy, then, marks the transition of Shakespeare's mind through the Congreve character of invention and dialogue ; that of lively and artificial brilliancy—a region in which he did not long loiter—

" But stoop'd to truth, and moraliz'd his song."

These remarks apply to the general contexture of the comedy, and the greater part of the dialogue. But it must not be overlooked that the whole is not the work of a mere boy. It had been played before Queen Elizabeth, according to the title-page of the edition of 1598, " this last Christmas," and, as it then shortly after appeared " newly corrected and augmented," it is probable that the author had followed the fashion of his times, when (according to Mr. Collier) " it was common for dramatists to revise and improve their plays, when they were selected for exhibition at court." It does not imply any great presumption of criticism, or demand peculiar delicacy of discrimination, to separate many of these acknowledged additions from the lighter and less valuable materials in which they are inserted. Rosaline's character of Biron in the second act, and her dialogue with him at the winding up of the drama, and Biron's speeches in the first and at the end of the fourth act, are among the passages which appropriate themselves at once to the period of the composition of the *Midsummer-Night's Dream* or the *Merchant of Venice*, not less in the mood of thought than in the peculiar poetic style and melody.

The story itself is but slight, the incidents few, and the higher characters, though varied, are but sketchily drawn — at least, taking the author's own maturer style of execution in that way as the standard. There was, therefore, no very great effort of original invention in either respect ; but whatever there is, either of plot or character, belongs to the author alone : for the diligence of the critics and antiquarians (Steevens, Skottowe, Collier, etc.) who have been most successful in tracing out the rough materials of romance, tradition, or history used by Shakespeare for the construction of his dramas, has entirely failed in discovering any thing of the kind in any older author, native or foreign, to which he could have been indebted on this occasion. It is well worthy of remark that Shakespeare, in his earlier works, bestowed more of the labour of invention upon his plot and incidents than he generally did afterwards, when he usually selected known personages, to whom and to the outline of whose story the popular mind was already somewhat familiar—thus, probably quite unconsciously, adopting from his own experience the usage of the great Greek dramatists. It may be that the impress of reality, which the circumstance of familiar names and events lends to the drama, more than compensated for any pleasure that mere novelty of incident could give either to the author or his audience. But, in his characters of broad humour, Shakespeare is here, as he always is, original and inventive. Although the Pedant and the Braggart are characters familiar to the old Italian stage, yet if the drama-

tist derived the general notion of such personages, as fitted
for stage-effect, from any Italian source (for the presumption
is but remote), still he assuredly painted them and their
affectations from the life ; these being characters, as Coleridge justly observes, which "a country town and a schoolboy's observation might supply."

All the personages of broader humour, in spite of their
extravagances and droll absurdities, have still an air of truth,
a solidity of effect, which at once indicates that, however
heightened and exaggerated, still they came upon the stage
from the real world, and not from the author's fancy; and
this solidity and reality tend to give a more unreal and
shadowy tone to the other and more courtly and poetic personages of the comedy. Such a remark can apply only to
Shakespeare's very early dramatic works. The other comic
creations of the second stage of the poet's career—Launcelot Gobbo, or Falstaff—do not command the temporary illu-
sion of the stage more than the nobler personages with whom
they are contrasted. Juliet is as true and real as her Nurse.

[*From Knight's " Pictorial Shakspere."* *]

Charles Lamb was wont to call *Love's Labour 's Lost* the
Comedy of Leisure. 'T is certain that in the commonwealth
of King Ferdinand of Navarre we have,

> "all men idle, all ;
> And women too."

The courtiers, in their pursuit of " that angel knowledge,"
waste their time in subtle contentions, how that angel is to
be won; the ladies from France spread their pavilions in
the sunny park, and there keep up their round of jokes with
their " wit's peddler," Boyet, " the nice ;" Armado listens
to his page while he warbles " Concolinel ;" Jaquenetta,
though she is " allowed for the dey," seems to have no dairy

* *Pictorial Edition of Shakspere*, edited by Charles Knight (2d ed.
London, 1867), vol. ii. of *Comedies*, p. 130 fol.

to look after; Costard acts as if he were neither plough-man nor swineherd, and born for no other work than to laugh forever at Moth, and, in the excess of his love for that "pathetical nit," to exclaim, "An I had but one penny in the world, thou shouldst have it to buy gingerbread;" the schoolmaster appears to be without scholars, the curate without a cure, the constable without watch and ward. There is, indeed, one parenthesis of real business connect-ed with the progress of the action—the difference between France and Navarre, in the matter of Aquitaine. But the settlement of this business is deferred till "to-morrow"—the "packet of specialities" is not come; and whether Aquitaine goes back to France, or the hundred thousand crowns return to Navarre, we never learn. This matter, then, being post-poned till a more fitting season, the whole set abandon themselves to what Dr. Johnson calls "strenuous idleness." The king and his courtiers forswear their studies, and every man becomes a lover and a sonneteer; the refined traveller of Spain resigns himself to his passion for the dairy-maid; the schoolmaster and the curate talk learnedly after dinner; and, at last, the king, the nobles, the priest, the pedant, the braggart, the page, and the clown join in one dance of mum-mery, in which they all laugh, and are laughed at. But still all this idleness is too energetic to warrant us in calling this the Comedy of Leisure. Let us try again. Is it not the Comedy of Affectations?

Molière, in his *Précieuses Ridicules*, has admirably hit off *one* affectation that had found its way into the private life of his own times. The ladies aspired to be wooed after the fashion of the Grand Cyrus. Madelon will be called Poli-xène, and Cathos Aminte. They dismiss their plain honest lovers, because marriage ought to be at the end of the ro-mance, and not at the beginning. They dote upon Masca-rille (the disguised lackey) when he assures them "Les gens de qualité savent tout sans avoir jamais rien appris."

They are in ecstasies at every thing. Madelon is "furieuse-ment pour les portraits;" Cathos loves "terriblement les énigmes." Even Mascarille's ribbon is "furieusement bien choisi;" his gloves "sentent terriblement bons;" and his feathers are "effroyablement belles." But in the *Pré-cieuses Ridicules*, Molière, as we have said, dealt with one affectation; in *Love's Labour's Lost* Shakspere presents us almost every variety of affectation that is founded upon a misdirection of intellectual activity. We have here many of the forms in which cleverness is exhibited as opposed to wis-dom, and false refinement as opposed to simplicity. The affected characters, even the most fantastical, are not fools; but, at the same time, the natural characters, who, in this play, are chiefly the women, have their intellectual foibles. All the modes of affectation are developed in one continued stream of fun and drollery; every one is laughing at the folly of the other, and the laugh grows louder and louder as the more natural characters, one by one, trip up the heels of the more affected. The most affected at last join in the laugh with the most natural; and the whole comes down to "plain kersey yea and nay"—from the syntax of Holofernes, and the "fire-new words" of Armado, to "greasy Joan" and "roasted crabs."

[*From Dowden's "Shakspere."* *]

Love's Labour's Lost, if we do not assign that place to *The Two Gentlemen of Verona*, is the first independent, wholly original work of Shakspere. Mr. Charles Knight named it "The Comedy of Affectations," and that title aptly interprets one intention of the play. It is a satirical extravaganza embodying Shakspere's criticism upon con-temporary fashions and foibles in speech, in manners, and in literature. This probably, more than any other of the plays

* *Shakspere: a Critical Study of his Mind and Art*, by Edward Dow-den; Harper's ed. p. 55 fol.

of Shakspere, suffers through lapse of time. Fantastical speech, pedantic learning, extravagant love-hyperbole, frigid fervours in poetry—against each of these, with the brightness and vivacity of youth, confident in the success of its cause, Shakspere directs the light artillery of his wit. Being young and clever, he is absolutely devoid of respect for nonsense, whether it be dainty, affected nonsense, or grave, unconscious nonsense.

But, over and above this, there is a serious intention in the play. It is a protest against youthful schemes of shaping life according to notions rather than according to reality, a protest against idealizing away the facts of life. The play is chiefly interesting as containing Shakspere's confession of faith with respect to the true principles of self-culture. The King of Navarre and his young lords had resolved, for a definite period of time, to circumscribe their beings and their lives with a little code of rules. They had designed to enclose a little favoured park in which ideas should rule to the exclusion of the blind and rude forces of nature. They were pleased to rearrange human character and human life, so that it might accord with their idealistic scheme of self-development. The court was to be a little Academe ; no woman was to be looked at for the space of three years ; food and sleep were to be placed under precise regulation. And the result is—what? That human nature refuses to be dealt with in this fashion of arbitrary selection and rejection. The youthful idealists had supposed that they would form a little group of select and refined ascetics of knowledge and culture ; it was quickly proved that they were men. The play is Shakspere's declaration in favour of the fact as it is. Here, he says, we are with such and such appetites and passions. Let us, in any scheme of self-development, get *that* fact acknowledged at all events ; otherwise we shall quickly enough betray ourselves as arrant fools, fit to be flouted by women, and needing to learn from them a portion of their directness, practicality, and good-sense.

And yet the Princess and Rosaline and Maria have not the entire advantage on their side. It is well to be practical, but to be practical, and also to have a capacity for ideas, is better. Berowne, the exponent of Shakspere's own thought, who entered into the youthful, idealistic project of his friends, with a satisfactory assurance that the time would come when the entire dream-structure would tumble ridiculously about the ears of them all—Berowne is yet a larger nature than the Princess or Rosaline. *His* good-sense is the good-sense of a thinker and of a man of action. When he is most flouted and bemocked, we yet acknowledge him victorious and the master ; and Rosaline will confess the fact by-and-by.

In the midst of merriment and nonsense comes a sudden and grievous incursion of fact full of pain. The father of the Princess is dead. All the world is not mirth—"this side is Hiems, Winter ; this Ver, the Spring." The lovers must part—"Jack hath not his Jill ;" and to engrave the lesson deeply, which each heart needs, the King and two of his companions are dismissed for a twelvemonth to learn the difference between reality and unreality ; while Berowne, who has known the mirth of the world, must also make acquaintance with its sorrow, must visit the speechless sick and try to win "the pained impotent to smile."

Let us get hold of the realities of human nature and human life, Shakspere would say, and let us found upon these realities, and not upon the mist or the air, our schemes of individual and social advancement. Not that Shakspere is hostile to culture ; but he knows that a perfect education must include the culture, through actual experience, of the senses and of the affections.

[*From Charles Cowden-Clarke's "Shakespeare-Characters."* *]

Charles Armitage Brown, in his clever volume upon the *Autobiographical Poems of Shakespeare*, pronounces that our

* From the *unpublished* "Second Series" of the *Shakespeare-Characters* (see 2 *Hen. IV.* p. 18), through the kindness of Mrs. Mary Cowden-Clarke.

poet's purpose in constructing the comedy of *Love's Labour 's Lost* was to satirize the fantastic gallantry of his age, and he adds : " As such, it must have been understood in his day, and keenly so ; and it is our business to understand it in the same way, or confine ourselves to those passages of elegant language and eloquence which he has brought forward as contrasts to the rest." It is probable that this may have been Shakespeare's intention ; and if so, he has performed his task in the pure spirit of his own gentle nature, for a more meek and unoffending satire never was penned. The whole play is like one of the high-flown romances of that age dramatized ; Sir Philip Sidney might have written it. It is a play consisting almost solely of conversation ; for the plot (if plot it can be called where plot is none, but a mere peg whereon to hang the dialogue) consists simply in a young king of Navarre and his three attendant lords and fellow-scholars entering into a compact for three years, under severe penalty, to live a life of seclusion, and to talk with no woman during that term. A princess of France, however, with her three lady attendants, comes on an embassy from her father to demand an interview with the king ; and the consequence is, that all the gentlemen, one after the other, break their compact, and fall fathoms deep in love with the fair missionaries. . . .

The play I have uniformly found to be a favourite with scholarly men ; not so much, as it should seem, for the choice language in the serious love-scenes, as for the solemn humour in the Spaniard, and the broad caricature in the pedagogue ; both of which, though really amusing, clearly betray the stamp of youth in the invention, as well as in their lineaments of character. The earnestness in the tone of gallantry put into the mouth of the young lord Biron (who, by the way, is an elegant, and, in every sense, a perfect squire of dames) is another corroboration of the play having been an early production of Shakespeare's ; and lastly, a great portion of the dialogue being written in doggerel verse, and much of it even in alternate rhymes, and which we find only in his acknowledged early plays, and rarely in those that are proved to be the production of his latter years, all confirm the belief as to its date.

There is little or no variety in the principal characters; hence, there is no ground for critical disquisition, or for notice of intellectual discrimination. The King, Ferdinand, has nothing regal in his deportment, but is really a social companion to Dumain, Longaville, and Biron, who call themselves his attendants; and they are all like birds of one nest, only Biron is the strongest in song,—and a happy brood of Arcadians they all are.

The princess, too, and her attendants are of the like class, and worthy to be mated with beings who led a life of unoffending gayety and mirth, and who might have brought back the golden age, when their first parents held the fee-simple of Eden. . . .

The whole company—Holofernes and all—vie with each other in

> "Taffeta phrases, silken terms precise,
> Three-pil'd hyperboles, spruce affectation,
> Figures pedantical."

The youngster, Moth, with that clear-sightedness with which quick children perceive the foibles of their elders, says of them, that "they have been at a great feast of languages, and stolen the scraps." The shrewd young rogue—"that handful of wit," as Costard calls him—has "purchased his little experience by his penny of observation." He is of the fresh age to relish a joke, and with the best effect to fan the flame of his master's affectation and conceit; and which would come with weaker effect from an elder hand. It is noticeable that Shakespeare has frequently brought grave and mirthful characters into juxtaposition, as if willing (and from preference) to show the latter in advantageous comparison with the staid virtue : witness Jaques and the other foresters ; Antonio and **Gratiano** ; Malvolio and Maria. So here the grave pomposity of Don Adriano de Armado is amusingly brought in contrasted combination with his whipper-snapper little page. The Don is a Spaniard, with all the gravity of his nation, and all the tardiness and deliberation of his race. The non-dispatch in the Spanish character has been proverbial for centuries. Bacon, in one of his Essays, quotes a common saying of the time to that effect: "Mi venga la muerte de Spagna" (May my death come from Spain). Armado has also all the fashionable gravity of a courtier, attached to a monarch who patronizes studiousness ; and all the fantastic solemnity of an affectation that chooses to fancy itself sublimely enamoured of a damsel of low degree. Jaquenetta is another Dulcinea del Toboso. The Hidalgo is fathoms deep in love, as the Knight of la Mancha adores his peasant wench, exalting her into the beacon, the cynosure of all his cogitations. Against the high-flown fantasies and didactic flourishes of Armado, the snapping, lap-dog repartees of his page come with as agreeable as whimsical effect ; of which their opening colloquy (the second scene of the first act) is a choice specimen.

Sir Nathaniel the curate, and Holofernes the school-master, furnish a signal proof of the foolery of pedantry. But they are not altogether so much natural fools as voluntary fools ; or, at any rate, fools of their own making. They are not born fools, but bred fools. They are blockheads of learning,—dolts of erudition,—oafs of knowledge,—the fools of pedantry. Quaint old Montaigne, talking of pedantic acquisition, asks naïvely: "What is the use of having our paunch full of meat, if it do not digest, and become part of us, and augment and strengthen us?" and he maintains that "time lost in pedantic study is worse than time idled away playing at ball ; for that, at least, animates the body, whereas, in the other case, all that his Latin and Greek has done for a lad is to render him more silly and presumptuous than he was before he left home." So with our two quacks of learning; they are intensely vain of their hoard of useless rubbish. They pride themselves, and in no stinted terms, upon the conscious possession of it; they lose no opportunity of heaping additions to its store, and neglect no occasion of displaying its extent. They laud themselves; they begaum each other; and they disdain everybody besides. Holofernes exclaims of Dull the constable: "Twice-sod simplicity, *bis coctus !* O thou monster ignorance, how deformed dost thou look!" And Sir Nathaniel rejoins complacently: "Sir, he hath never fed of the dainties that are bred in a book; he hath not eat paper, as it were; he hath not drunk ink; his intellect is not replenished; he is only an animal, only sensible in the duller parts; and such barren plants are set before us, that we thankful should be (which we of taste and feeling are) for those parts that do fructify in us more than he."

Delectable fructification truly, if these be the fruits of book-learning! This is the very quintessence of conceit and complacency.

That is a rich bout at nonsense-fun where the two owls are indulging their pedantical rodomontade: Holofernes spouting like a conduit; Sir Nathaniel dotingly aping him, and even noting down some of his favourite flourishes, that he may, upon occasion, sport them himself; while three more oddities arrive upon the scene, heaping up the absurdity. The Spanish solemnity of Don Armado, the childish pertness of little Moth, and the boorish humour of Costard come into ludicrous conjunction with the learned foolery of the two others; while the whole is crowned by the dense fog of goodman Dull's obtuseness, who has neither "spoken" nor "understood" one "word all this while," but who thinks he might "make one in a dance or so," or perchance "play on the tabor to the Worthies, and let them dance the hay."

There is an exuberance, an extravagance in Shakespeare's fun which is infectious. We laugh in spite of ourselves, as it were; stung by that keen sense of the ludicrous, which has evidently smitten and inspired the writer. We feel, in reading Shakespeare's drollery, that he himself had a relish for it; that he enjoyed a frolic of words; that he loved a bout of jesting; that he revelled in a spell of waggery and nonsense: "Most nonsense, best sense," as beloved Charles Lamb said. One of the poet's critics has well said that "in no one point, perhaps, does he exaggerate but in laughter." There is a hearty, outpouring, overflowing flood in Shakespeare's laughter, which, like laughter with an intimate friend, is at once irresistible in sympathy, and deliciously wholesome in its freedom and light-hearted abandonment. We are the better for such laughter; we are the better for an explosive, unrestrained shout with a friend, or with such a friend-book as Shakespeare's, such a friend-writer as Shakespeare himself. After we have steeped our souls in his profound truths, and saturated our minds with his sublime wisdom, we may recreate our spirits with his humorous pictures, and refresh our hearts with his cordial, genial images. We may learn from him, gravely, studiously, profitably; and we may, after, laugh with him, gayly, mirthfully, joyously, even to the very tip-top of hilarious, tear-provoking laughter; and still with profit to ourselves. For few things have we more cause to be grateful than for a true and genuine source of true and genuine laughter. Laughter beautifies the human face, it irradiates the countenance, it lights up the eyes in lustrous sparkles, it dimples the mouth, it moulds plainest features into comeliness and grace. It cheers and sweetens the temper, it invigorates and animates the frame. It diminishes ills, it lightens care, it softens trouble. It casts petty annoyances into shade and oblivion; it destroys wrath, and kills vexation. For such benefits as these, among a legion of others, have we to thank Shakespeare; since the laughter that he furnishes—like all else that his pages supply—is matchless of its kind.

LOVE'S LABOUR 'S LOST.

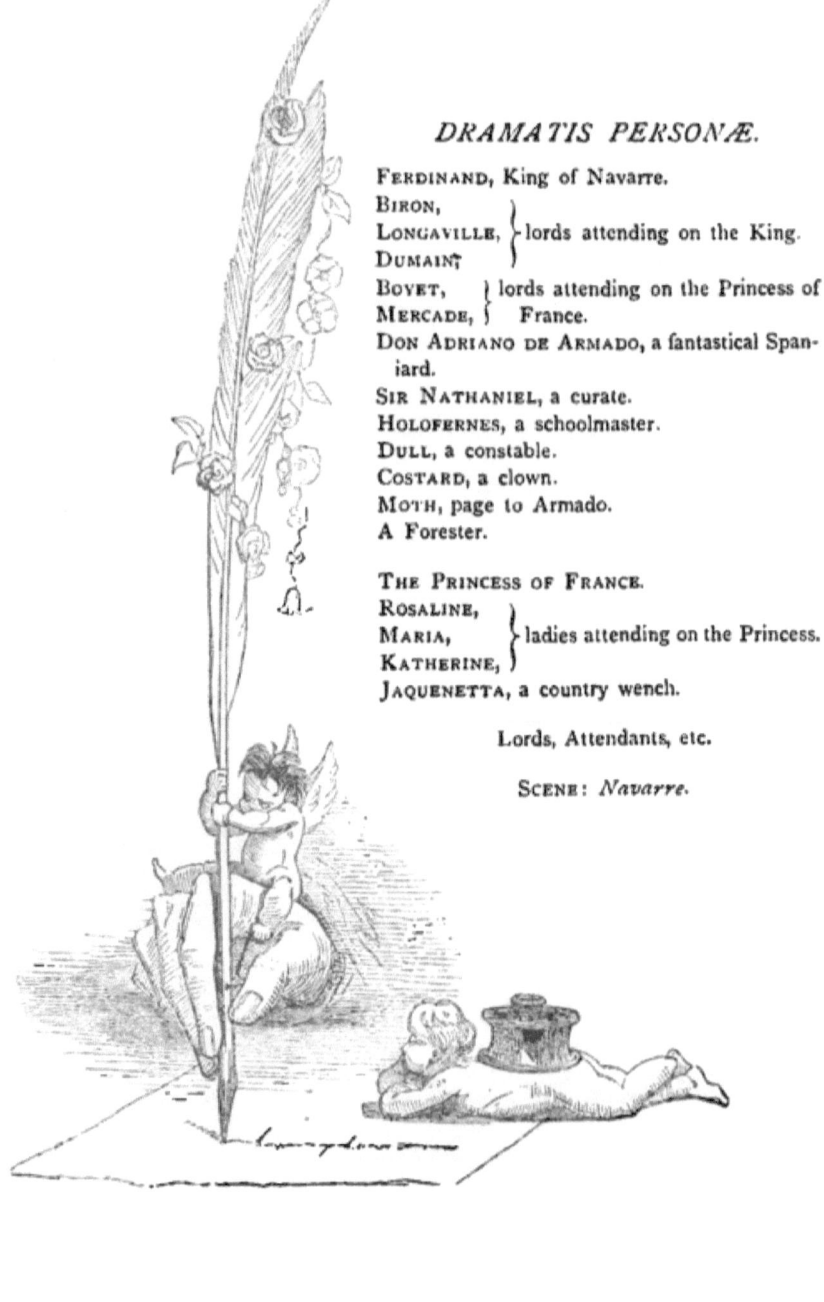

DRAMATIS PERSONÆ.

FERDINAND, King of Navarre.

BIRON,
LONGAVILLE, } lords attending on the King.
DUMAIN,

BOYET, } lords attending on the Princess of
MERCADE, } France.

DON ADRIANO DE ARMADO, a fantastical Spaniard.

SIR NATHANIEL, a curate.

HOLOFERNES, a schoolmaster.

DULL, a constable.

COSTARD, a clown.

MOTH, page to Armado.

A Forester.

THE PRINCESS OF FRANCE.

ROSALINE,
MARIA, } ladies attending on the Princess.
KATHERINE,

JAQUENETTA, a country wench.

Lords, Attendants, etc.

SCENE: *Navarre.*

Thy curious-knotted garden (i. 1. 237).

ACT I.

SCENE I. *The King of Navarre's Park.*

Enter FERDINAND, *King of* NAVARRE, BIRON, LONGAVILLE,
and DUMAIN.

King. Let fame, that all hunt after in their lives,
Live register'd upon our brazen tombs,
And then grace us in the disgrace of death;
When, spite of cormorant devouring Time,
The endeavour of this present breath may buy
That honour which shall bate his scythe's keen edge
And make us heirs of all eternity.
Therefore, brave conquerors,—for so you are,
That war against your own affections

And the huge army of the world's desires,—   10
Our late edict shall strongly stand in force.
Navarre shall be the wonder of the world;
Our court shall be a little Academe,
Still and contemplative in living art.
You three, Biron, Dumain, and Longaville,
Have sworn for three years' term to live with me
My fellow-scholars, and to keep those statutes
That are recorded in this schedule here.
Your oaths are pass'd; and now subscribe your names,
That his own hand may strike his honour down   20
That violates the smallest branch herein.
If you are arm'd to do as sworn to do,
Subscribe to your deep oaths, and keep it too.
    Longaville. I am resolv'd; 't is but a three years' fast:
The mind shall banquet, though the body pine.
Fat paunches have lean pates, and dainty bits
Make rich the ribs, but bankrupt quite the wits.
    Dumain. My loving lord, Dumain is mortified;
The grosser manner of these world's delights
He throws upon the gross world's baser slaves.   30
To love, to wealth, to pomp, I pine and die,
With all these living in philosophy.
    Biron. I can but say their protestation over;
So much, dear liege, I have already sworn,
That is, to live and study here three years.
But there are other strict observances;
As, not to see a woman in that term,
Which I hope well is not enrolled there;
And one day in a week to touch no food,
And but one meal on every day beside,   40
The which I hope is not enrolled there;
And then, to sleep but three hours in the night,
And not be seen to wink of all the day—
When I was wont to think no harm all night,

And make a dark night too of half the day—
Which I hope well is not enrolled there.
O, these are barren tasks, too hard to keep,
Not to see ladies, study, fast, not sleep !
   King. Your oath is pass'd to pass away from these.
   Biron. Let me say no, my liege, an if you please;   50
I only swore to study with your grace,
And stay here in your court for three years' space.
   Longaville. You swore to that, Biron, and to the rest.
   Biron. By yea and nay, sir, then I swore in jest.
What is the end of study ? let me know.
   King. Why, that to know which else we should not
      know.
   Biron. Things hid and barr'd, you mean, from common
      sense?
   King. Ay, that is study's godlike recompense.
   Biron. Come on, then ; I will swear to study so.
To know the thing I am forbid to know: 60
As thus,—to study where I well may dine,
   When I to feast expressly am forbid ;
Or study where to meet some mistress fine,
   When mistresses from common sense are hid ;
Or, having sworn too hard a keeping oath,
Study to break it and not break my troth.
If study's gain be thus, and this be so,
Study knows that which yet it doth not know.
Swear me to this, and I will ne'er say no.
   King. These be the stops that hinder study quite,   70
And train our intellects to vain delight.
   Biron. Why, all delights are vain ; and that most vain,
Which with pain purchas'd doth inherit pain :
As, painfully to pore upon a book
   To seek the light of truth, while truth the while
Doth falsely blind the eyesight of his look.
   Light seeking light doth light of light beguile ;

So, ere you find where light in darkness lies,
Your light grows dark by losing of your eyes.
Study me how to please the eye indeed   80
   By fixing it upon a fairer eye,
Who dazzling so, that eye shall be his heed,
   And give him light that it was blinded by.
Study is like the heaven's glorious sun,
   That will not be deep-search'd with saucy looks ;
Small have continual plodders ever won,
   Save base authority from others' books.
These earthly godfathers of heaven's lights,
   That give a name to every fixed star,
Have no more profit of their shining nights   90
   Than those that walk and wot not what they are.
Too much to know is to know nought but fame ;
And every godfather can give a name.
   King. How well he 's read, to reason against reading !
   Dumain. Proceeded well, to stop all good proceeding !
   Longaville. He weeds the corn and still lets grow the
      weeding.
   Biron. The spring is near when green geese are a-breeding.
   Dumain. How follows that ?
   Biron.   Fit in his place and time.
   Dumain. In reason nothing.
   Biron.   Something then in rhyme.
   King. Biron is like an envious sneaping frost   100
   That bites the first-born infants of the spring.
   Biron. Well, say I am ; why should proud summer boast
   Before the birds have any cause to sing ?
Why should I joy in an abortive birth?
   At Christmas I no more desire a rose
Than wish a snow in May's new-fangled mirth,
   But like of each thing that in season grows.
So you, to study now it is too late,
Climb o'er the house to unlock the little gate.

King. Well, sit you out : go home, Biron ; adieu ! 110
Biron. No, my good lord ; I have sworn to stay with you :
And though I have for barbarism spoke more
Than for that angel knowledge you can say,
Yet confident I 'll keep what I have swore,
And bide the penance of each three years' day.
Give me the paper : let me read the same ;
And to the strict'st decrees I 'll write my name.
King. How well this yielding rescues thee from shame !
Biron. [Reads] ' *Item, That no woman shall come within a
mile of my court :*' Hath this been proclaimed? 120
Longaville. Four days ago.
Biron. Let 's see the penalty. [Reads] ' *On pain of losing
her tongue.*'—Who devised this penalty?
Longaville. Marry, that did I.
Biron. Sweet lord, and why?
Longaville. To fright them hence with that dread penalty.
Biron. A dangerous law against gentility !
[Reads] ' *Item, If any man be seen to talk with a woman
within the term of three years, he shall endure such public shame
as the rest of the court can possibly devise.*' 130
This article, my liege, yourself must break ;
For well you know here comes in embassy
The French king's daughter with yourself to speak—
A maid of grace and complete majesty—
About surrender up of Aquitaine
To her decrepit, sick, and bedrid father :
Therefore this article is made in vain,
Or vainly comes the admired princess hither.
King. What say you, lords? why, this was quite forgot.
Biron. So study evermore is overshot. 140
While it doth study to have what it would,
It doth forget to do the thing it should ;
And when it hath the thing it hunteth most,
'T is won as towns with fire, so won, so lost.

King. We must of force dispense with this decree;
She must lie here on mere necessity.
    Biron. Necessity will make us all forsworn
Three thousand times within this three years' space;
For every man with his affects is born,
    Not by might master'd, but by special grace.   150
If I break faith, this word shall speak for me;
I am forsworn on mere necessity.—
So to the laws at large I write my name;   [*Subscribes.*
    And he that breaks them in the least degree
Stands in attainder of eternal shame.
    Suggestions are to others as to me;
But I believe, although I seem so loath,
I am, the last that will last keep his oath.
But is there no quick recreation granted?
    King. Ay, that there is. Our court, you know, is haunted
With a refined traveller of Spain;   161
A man in all the world's new fashion planted,
    That hath a mint of phrases in his brain;
One whom the music of his own vain tongue
    Doth ravish like enchanting harmony;
A man of complements, whom right and wrong
    Have chose as umpire of their mutiny.
This child of fancy that Armado hight
    For interim to our studies shall relate
In high-born words the worth of many a knight   170
    From tawny Spain lost in the world's debate.
How you delight, my lords, I know not, I,
But, I protest, I love to hear him lie,
And I will use him for my minstrelsy.
    Biron. Armado is a most illustrious wight,
A man of fire-new words, fashion's own knight.
    Longaville. Costard the swain and he shall be our sport;
And so to study, three years is but short.

Enter DULL *with a letter, and* COSTARD.

Dull. Which is the duke's own person?

Biron. This, fellow; what wouldst? 180

Dull. I myself reprehend his own person, for I am his grace's tharborough; but I would see his own person in flesh and blood.

Biron. This is he.

Dull. Signior Arme—Arme—commends you. There 's villany abroad; this letter will tell you more.

Costard. Sir, the contempts thereof are as touching me.

King. A letter from the magnificent Armado.

Biron. How low soever the matter, I hope in God for high words. 190

Longaville. A high hope for a low having; God grant us patience!

Biron. To hear? or forbear laughing?

Longaville. To hear meekly, sir, and to laugh moderately : or to forbear both.

Biron. Well, sir, be it as the style shall give us cause to climb in the merriness.

Costard. The matter is to me, sir, as concerning Jaquenetta. The manner of it is, I was taken with the manner.

Biron. In what manner? 200

Costard. In manner and form following, sir; all those three : I was seen with her in the manor-house, sitting with her upon the form, and taken following her into the park; which, put together, is in manner and form following. Now, sir, for the manner,—it is the manner of a man to speak to a woman; for the form,—in some form.

Biron. For the following, sir?

Costard. As it shall follow in my correction; and God defend the right!

King. Will you hear this letter with attention? 210

Biron. As we would hear an oracle.

Costard. Such is the simplicity of man to hearken after the flesh.

King. [Reads] '*Great deputy, the welkin's vicegerent and sole dominator of Navarre, my soul's earth's god, and body's fostering patron.*'

Costard. Not a word of Costard yet.

King. [Reads] '*So it is,*'—

Costard. It may be so ; but if he say it is so, he is, in telling true, but so.   220

King. Peace !

Costard. Be to me, and every man that dares not fight !

King. No words !

Costard. Of other men's secrets, I beseech you.

King. [Reads] '*So it is, besieged with sable-coloured melancholy, I did commend the black-oppressing humour to the most wholesome physic of thy health-giving air, and, as I am a gentleman, betook myself to walk. The time when? About the sixth hour; when beasts most graze, birds best peck, and men sit down to that nourishment which is called supper: so much for the time when. Now for the ground which; which, I mean, I walked upon: it is ycleped thy park. Then for the place where; where, I mean, I did encounter that obscene and most preposterous event, that draweth from my snow-white pen the ebon-coloured ink, which here thou viewest, beholdest, surveyest, or seest: but to the place where; it standeth north-north-east and by east from the west corner of thy curious-knotted garden: there did I see that low-spirited swain, that base minnow of thy mirth,*'—

Costard. Me.   240

King. [Reads] '*that unlettered small-knowing soul,*'—

Costard. Me.

King. [Reads] '*that shallow vassal,*'—

Costard. Still me.

King. [Reads] '*which, as I remember, hight Costard,*'—

Costard. O, me !

King. [Reads] '*sorted and consorted, contrary to thy estab-
lished proclaimed edict and continent canon, with—with—O,
with—but with this I passion to say wherewith,*'—

Costard. With a wench.   250

King. [Reads] '*with a child of our grandmother Eve, a female; or, for thy more sweet understanding, a woman. Him I,
as my ever-esteemed duty pricks me on, have sent to thee, to receive the meed of punishment, by thy sweet grace's officer, Anthony Dull, a man of good repute, carriage, bearing, and estimation.*'

Dull. Me, an 't shall please you; I am Anthony Dull.

King. [Reads] '*For Jaquenetta,—so is the weaker vessel
called which I apprehended with the aforesaid swain,—I keep
her as a vessel of thy law's fury, and shall, at the least of thy
sweet notice, bring her to trial. Thine, in all compliments of devoted and heart-burning heat of duty.*'   262

'DON ADRIANO DE ARMADO.'

Biron. This is not so well as I looked for, but the best
that ever I heard.

King. Ay, the best for the worst.—But, sirrah, what say
you to this?

Costard. Sir, I confess the wench.

King. Did you hear the proclamation?

Costard. I do confess much of the hearing it, but little of
the marking of it.   270

King. It was proclaimed a year's imprisonment, to be
taken with a wench.

Costard. I was taken with none, sir; I was taken with a
damosel.

King. Well, it was proclaimed damosel.

Costard. This was no damosel neither, sir; she was a virgin.

King. It is so varied too; for it was proclaimed virgin.

Costard. If it were, I deny her virginity; I was taken with
a maid.

King. This maid will not serve your turn, sir.   280

Costard. This maid will serve my turn, sir.

King. Sir, I will pronounce your sentence : you shall fast a week with bran and water.

Costard. I had rather pray a month with mutton and porridge.

King. And Don Armado shall be your keeper.—
My Lord Biron, see him deliver'd o'er ;—
And go we, lords, to put in practice that
Which each to other hath so strongly sworn.

                [Exeunt King, Longaville, and Dumain.

Biron. I 'll lay my head to any good man's hat,   290
These oaths and laws will prove an idle scorn.—
Sirrah, come on.

Costard. I suffer for the truth, sir; for true it is, I was taken with Jaquenetta, and Jaquenetta is a true girl ; and therefore welcome. the sour cup of prosperity ! Affliction may one day smile again ; and till then, sit thee down, sorrow !   *[Exeunt.*

SCENE II.   *Another Part of the Park.*

Enter ARMADO *and* MOTH.

Armado. Boy, what sign is it when a man of great spirit grows melancholy ?

Moth. A great sign, sir, that he will look sad.

Armado. Why, sadness is one and the selfsame thing, dear imp.

Moth. No, no; O Lord, sir, no !

Armado. How canst thou part sadness and melancholy, my tender juvenal ?

Moth. By a familiar demonstration of the working, my tough senior.   10

Armado. Why tough senior? why tough senior?

Moth. Why tender juvenal ? why tender juvenal ?

Armado. I spoke it, tender juvenal, as a congruent epitheton appertaining to thy young days, which we may nominate tender.

Moth. And I, tough senior, as an appertinent title to your old time, which we may name tough.

Armado. Pretty and apt.

Moth. How mean you, sir? I pretty, and my saying apt? or I apt, and my saying pretty? 20

Armado. Thou pretty, because little.

Moth. Little pretty, because little. Wherefore apt?

Armado. And therefore apt, because quick.

Moth. Speak you this in my praise, master?

Armado. In thy condign praise.

Moth. I will praise an eel with the same praise.

Armado. What, that an eel is ingenious?

Moth. That an eel is quick.

Armado. I do say thou art quick in answers; thou heatest my blood. 30

Moth. I am answered, sir.

Armado. I love not to be crossed.

Moth. [*Aside*] He speaks the mere contrary; crosses love not him.

Armado. I have promised to study three years with the duke.

Moth. You may do it in an hour, sir.

Armado. Impossible.

Moth. How many is one thrice told?

Armado. I am ill at reckoning; it fitteth the spirit of a tapster. 40

Moth. You are a gentleman and a gamester, sir.

Armado. I confess both; they are both the varnish of a complete man.

Moth. Then, I am sure, you know how much the gross sum of deuce-ace amounts to.

Armado. It doth amount to one more than two.

Moth. Which the base vulgar do call three.

Armado. True.

Moth. Why, sir, is this such a piece of study? Now here is three studied, ere you 'll thrice wink; and how easy it is to put years to the word three, and study three years in two words, the dancing horse will tell you. 52

Armado. A most fine figure!

Moth. [*Aside*] To prove you a cipher.

Armado. I will hereupon confess I am in love; and as it is base for a soldier to love, so am I in love with a base wench. If drawing my sword against the humour of affection would deliver me from the reprobate thought of it, I would take desire prisoner, and ransom him to any French courtier for a new-devised courtesy. I think scorn to sigh; methinks I should outswear Cupid. Comfort me, boy. What great men have been in love? 62

Moth. Hercules, master.

Armado. Most sweet Hercules!—More authority, dear boy, name more; and, sweet my child, let them be men of good repute and carriage.

Moth. Samson, master: he was a man of good carriage, great carriage, for he carried the town-gates on his back like a porter; and he was in love. 69

Armado. O well-knit Samson! strong-jointed Samson! I do excel thee in my rapier as much as thou didst me in carrying gates. I am in love too.—Who was Samson's love, my dear Moth?

Moth. A woman, master.

Armado. Of what complexion?

Moth. Of all the four, or the three, or the two, or one of the four.

Armado. Tell me precisely of what complexion.

Moth. Of the sea-water green, sir.

Armado. Is that one of the four complexions? 80

Moth. As I have read, sir; and the best of them too.

Armado. Green indeed is the colour of lovers; but to have a love of that colour, methinks Samson had small reason for it. He surely affected her for her wit.

Moth. It was so, sir; for she had a green wit.

Armado. My love is most immaculate white and red.

Moth. Most maculate thoughts, master, are masked under such colours.

Armado. Define, define, well-educated infant.

Moth. My father's wit and my mother's tongue, assist me!

Armado. Sweet invocation of a child; most pretty and pathetical!   92

Moth. If she be made of white and red,
    Her faults will ne'er be known,
For blushing cheeks by faults are bred
    And fears by pale white shown;
Then if she fear, or be to blame,
    By this you shall not know,
For still her cheeks possess the same
    Which native she doth owe.   100

A dangerous rhyme, master, against the reason of white and red.

Armado. Is there not a ballad, boy, of the King and the Beggar?

Moth. The world was very guilty of such a ballad some three ages since, but I think now 't is not to be found; or, if it were, it would neither serve for the writing nor the tune.

Armado. I will have that subject newly writ o'er, that I may example my digression by some mighty precedent. Boy, I do love that country girl that I took in the park with the rational hind Costard; she deserves well.   111

Moth. [*Aside*] To be whipped,—and yet a better love than my master.

Armado. Sing, boy; my spirit grows heavy in love.

Moth. And that's great marvel, loving a light wench.

Armado. I say, sing.

Moth. Forbear till this company be past.

Enter DULL, COSTARD, *and* JAQUENETTA.

Dull. Sir, the duke's pleasure is, that you keep Costard

safe; and you must let him take no delight nor no penance, but he must fast three days a week. For this damsel, I must keep her at the park; she is allowed for the day-woman. Fare you well.   122

Armado. I do betray myself with blushing.—Maid!

Jaquenetta. Man!

Armado. I will visit thee at the lodge.

Jaquenetta. That 's hereby.

Armado. I know where it is situate.

Jaquenetta. Lord, how wise you are!

Armado. I will tell thee wonders.

Jaquenetta. With that face?   130

Armado. I love thee.

Jaquenetta. So I heard you say.

Armado. And so, farewell.

Jaquenetta. Fair weather after you!

Dull. Come, Jaquenetta, away!

                    [*Exeunt Dull and Jaquenetta.*

Armado. Villain, thou shalt fast for thy offences ere thou be pardoned.

Costard. Well, sir, I hope, when I do it, I shall do it on a full stomach.

Armado. Thou shalt be heavily punished.   140

Costard. I am more bound to you than your fellows, for they are but lightly rewarded.

Armado. Take away this villain; shut him up.

Moth. Come, you transgressing slave; away!

Costard. Let me not be pent up, sir; I will fast, being loose.

Moth. No, sir; that were fast and loose: thou shalt to prison.

Costard. Well, if ever I do see the merry days of desolation that I have seen, some shall see—   150

Moth. What shall some see?

Costard. Nay, nothing, Master Moth, but what they look

upon.   It is not for prisoners to be too silent in their words ;
and therefore I will say nothing.   I thank God I have
as little patience as another man, and therefore I can be
quiet.   [*Exeunt Moth and Costard.*

   Armado. I do affect the very ground, which is base, where
her shoe, which is baser, guided by her foot, which is basest,
doth tread.   I shall be forsworn, which is a great argument
of falsehood, if I love.   And how can that be true love which
is falsely attempted?   Love is a familiar ; Love is a devil :
there is no evil angel but Love.   Yet was Samson so tempted, and he had an excellent strength ; yet was Solomon so
seduced, and he had a very good wit.   Cupid's butt-shaft is
too hard for Hercules' club, and therefore too much odds
for a Spaniard's rapier.   The first and second cause will
not serve my turn ; the passado he respects not, the duello
he regards not : his disgrace is to be called boy, but his glory
is to subdue men.   Adieu, valour ! rust, rapier ! be still, drum !
for your manager is in love ; yea, he loveth.   Assist me, some
extemporal god of rhyme, for I am sure I shall turn sonnet.
Devise, wit ! write, pen ! for I am for whole volumes in folio.
                                                      [*Exit.*

D

ACT II.

SCENE I. *The Park. A Pavilion and Tents at a Distance.*

Enter the PRINCESS OF FRANCE, ROSALINE, MARIA, KATHE-
RINE, BOYET, Lords, *and other* Attendants.

Boyet. Now, madam, summon up your dearest spirits.
Consider who the king your father sends,
To whom he sends, and what 's his embassy:
Yourself, held precious in the world's esteem,
To parley with the sole inheritor
Of all perfections that a man may owe,
Matchless Navarre; the plea of no less weight
Than Aquitaine, a dowry for a queen.
Be now as prodigal of all dear grace
As Nature was in making graces dear,   10
When she did starve the general world beside
And prodigally gave them all to you.
   Princess. Good Lord Boyet, my beauty, though but mean,

Needs not the painted flourish of your praise ;
Beauty is bought by judgment of the eye,
Not utter'd by base sale of chapmen's tongues.
I am less proud to hear you tell my worth
Than you much willing to be counted wise
In spending your wit in the praise of mine.
But now to task the tasker: good Boyet,   20
You are not ignorant, all-telling fame
Doth noise abroad, Navarre hath made a vow,
Till painful study shall outwear three years,
No woman may approach his silent court.
Therefore to 's seemeth it a needful course,
Before we enter his forbidden gates,
To know his pleasure ; and in that behalf,
Bold of your worthiness, we single you
As our best-moving fair solicitor.
Tell him, the daughter of the King of France,   30
On serious business, craving quick dispatch,
Importunes personal conference with his grace.
Haste, signify so much ; while we attend,
Like humble-visag'd suitors, his high will.
    Boyet. Proud of employment, willingly I go.
    Princess. All pride is willing pride, and yours is so.—
                           [Exit Boyet.

Who are the votaries, my loving lords,
That are vow-fellows with this virtuous duke?
    1 *Lord.* Lord Longaville is one.
    Princess.   Know you the man ?
    Maria. I know him, madam ; at a marriage-feast,   40
Between Lord Perigort and the beauteous heir
Of Jaques Falconbridge, solemnized
In Normandy, saw I this Longaville.
A man of sovereign parts he is esteem'd ;
Well fitted in the arts, glorious in arms:
Nothing becomes him ill that he would well.

The only soil of his fair virtue's gloss—
If virtue's gloss will stain with any soil—
Is a sharp wit match'd with too blunt a will ;
Whose edge hath power to cut, whose will still wills   50
It should none spare that come within his power.
    Princess. Some merry mocking lord, belike ; is 't so?
    Maria. They say so most that most his humours know.
    Princess. Such short-liv'd wits do wither as they grow.
Who are the rest?
    Katherine. The young Dumain, a well-accomplish'd youth,
Of all that virtue love for virtue lov'd ;
Most power to do most harm, least knowing ill,
For he hath wit to make an ill shape good,
And shape to win grace though he had no wit.   60
I saw him at the Duke Alençon's once ;
And much too little of that good I saw
Is my report to his great worthiness.
    Rosaline. Another of these students at that time
Was there with him, if I have heard a truth.
Biron they call him ; but a merrier man,
Within the limit of becoming mirth,
I never spent an hour's talk withal.
His eye begets occasion for his wit ;
For every object that the one doth catch   70
The other turns to a mirth-moving jest,
Which his fair tongue, conceit's expositor,
Delivers in such apt and gracious words
That aged ears play truant at his tales
And younger hearings are quite ravished,
So sweet and voluble is his discourse,
    Princess. God bless my ladies! are they all in love,
That every one her own hath garnished
With such bedecking ornaments of praise?
    1 *Lord.* Here comes Boyet.

Re-enter BOYET.

Princess.   Now, what admittance, lord?   80

Boyet. Navarre had notice of your fair approach,
And he and his competitors in oath
Were all address'd to meet you, gentle lady,
Before I came.   Marry, thus much I have learnt:
He rather means to lodge you in the field,
Like one that comes here to besiege his court,
Than seek a dispensation for his oath,
To let you enter his unpeopled house.—
Here comes Navarre.

Enter KING, LONGAVILLE, DUMAIN, BIRON, *and* Attendants.

King. Fair princess, welcome to the court of Navarre.   90

Princess. Fair I give you back again, and welcome I have
not yet ; the roof of this court is too high to be yours, and
welcome to the wide fields too base to be mine.

King. You shall be welcome, madam, to my court.

Princess. I will be welcome, then ; conduct me thither.

King. Hear me, dear lady ; I have sworn an oath.

Princess. Our Lady help my lord ! he 'll be forsworn.

King. Not for the world, fair madam, by my will.

Princess. Why, will shall break it ; will and nothing else.

King. Your ladyship is ignorant what it is.   100

Princess. Were my lord so, his ignorance were wise,
Where now his knowledge must prove ignorance.
I hear your grace hath sworn out house-keeping ;
'T is deadly sin to keep that oath, my lord,
And sin to break it.
But pardon me, I am too sudden-bold ;
To teach a teacher ill beseemeth me.
Vouchsafe to read the purpose of my coming,
And suddenly resolve me in my suit.

King. Madam, I will, if suddenly I may.   110

Princess. You will the sooner that I were away,
For you 'll prove perjur'd if you make me stay.
   Biron. Did not I dance with you in Brabant once?
   Rosaline. Did not I dance with you in Brabant once?
   Biron. I know you did.
   Rosaline. How needless was it then to ask the question!
   Biron. You must not be so quick.
   Rosaline. 'T is long of you that spur me with such questions.
   Biron. Your wit 's too hot, it speeds too fast, 't will tire.
   Rosaline. Not till it leave the rider in the mire.   120
   Biron. What time o' day?
   Rosaline. The hour that fools should ask.
   Biron. Now fair befall your mask!
   Rosaline. Fair fall the face it covers!
   Biron. And send you many lovers!
   Rosaline. Amen, so you be none.
   Biron. Nay, then will I be gone.
   King. Madam, your father here doth intimate
The payment of a hundred thousand crowns;
Being but the one half of an entire sum   130
Disbursed by my father in his wars.
But say that he or we, as neither have,
Receiv'd that sum, yet there remains unpaid
A hundred thousand more; in surety of the which,
One part of Aquitaine is bound to us,
Although not valued to the money's worth.
If then the king your father will restore
But that one half which is unsatisfied,
We will give up our right in Aquitaine,
And hold fair friendship with his majesty.   140
But that, it seems, he little purposeth,
For here he doth demand to have repaid
A hundred thousand crowns; and not demands,
On payment of a hundred thousand crowns,

To have his title live in Aquitaine ;
Which we much rather had depart withal,
And have the money by our father lent,
Than Aquitaine so gelded as it is.
Dear princess, were not his requests so far
From reason's yielding, your fair self should make   150
A yielding 'gainst some reason in my breast,
And go well satisfied to France again.
    Princess. You do the king my father too much wrong,
And wrong the reputation of your name,
In so unseeming to confess receipt
Of that which hath so faithfully been paid.
    King. I do protest I never heard of it ;
And if you prove it, I 'll repay it back
Or yield up Aquitaine.
    Princess.   We arrest your word.—
Boyet, you can produce acquittances   160
For such a sum from special officers
Of Charles his father.
    King.   Satisfy me so.
    Boyet. So please your grace, the packet is not come
Where that and other specialties are bound ;
To-morrow you shall have a sight of them.
    King. It shall suffice me ; at which interview
All liberal reason I will yield unto.
Meantime receive such welcome at my hand
As honour without breach of honour may
Make tender of to thy true worthiness.   170
You may not come, fair princess, in my gates ;
But here without you shall be so receiv'd
As you shall deem yourself lodg'd in my heart,
Though so denied fair harbour in my house.
Your own good thoughts excuse me, and farewell ;
To-morrow shall we visit you again.
    Princess. Sweet health and fair desires consort your grace !

King. Thy own wish wish I thee in every place! [*Exit.*

Biron. Lady, I will commend you to mine own heart.

Rosaline. Pray you, do my commendations; I would be glad to see it.　181

Biron. I would you heard it groan.

Rosaline. Is the fool sick?

Biron. Sick at the heart.

Rosaline. Alack, let it blood.

Biron. Would that do it good?

Rosaline. My physic says ay.

Biron. Will you prick 't with your eye?

Rosaline. No point, with my knife.

Biron. Now, God save thy life!　190

Rosaline. And yours from long living!

Biron. I cannot stay thanksgiving.　　　　[*Retiring.*

Dumain. Sir, I pray you, a word: what lady is that same?

Boyet. The heir of Alençon, Katherine her name.

Dumain. A gallant lady.　Monsieur, fare you well. [*Exit.*

Longaville. I beseech you a word: what is she in the white?

Boyet. A woman sometimes, an you saw her in the light.

Longaville. Perchance light in the light.　I desire her name.

Boyet. She hath but one for herself; to desire that were a shame.

Longaville. Pray you, sir, whose daughter?　200

Boyet. Her mother's, I have heard.

Longaville. God's blessing on your beard!

Boyet. Good sir, be not offended.
She is an heir of Falconbridge.

Longaville. Nay, my choler is ended.
She is a most sweet lady.

Boyet. Not unlike, sir, that may be.　　　[*Exit Longaville.*

Biron. What 's her name in the cap?

Boyet. Rosaline, by good hap.

Biron. Is she wedded or no?　210

Boyet. To her will, sir, or so.

Biron. You are welcome, sir; adieu.

Boyet. Farewell to me, sir, and welcome to you.

　　　　　　　　　　　　　　　　　[Exit Biron.

Maria. That last is Biron, the merry mad-cap lord;
Not a word with him but a jest.

Boyet.　　　　　　　　　And every jest but a word.

Princess. It was well done of you to take him at his word.

Boyet. I was as willing to grapple as he was to board.

Maria. Two hot sheeps, marry.

Boyet.　　　　　　　　　And wherefore not ships?
No sheep, sweet lamb, unless we feed on your lips.

Maria. You sheep, and I pasture; shall that finish the
　　jest?　　　　　　　　　　　　　　　　　220

Boyet. So you grant pasture for me. *[Offering to kiss her.*

Maria.　　　　　　　　　Not so, gentle beast;
My lips are no common, though several they be.

Boyet. Belonging to whom?

Maria.　　　　　　　　　To my fortunes and me.

Princess. Good wits will be jangling; but, gentles, agree.
This civil war of wits were much better us'd
On Navarre and his book-men, for here 't is abus'd.

Boyet. If my observation, which very seldom lies,
By the heart's still rhetoric disclosed with eyes,
Deceive me not now, Navarre is infected.

Princess. With what?　　　　　　　　　230

Boyet. With that which we lovers entitle affected.

Princess. Your reason?

Boyet. Why, all his behaviours did make their retire
To the court of his eye, peeping thorough desire;
His heart, like an agate, with your print impress'd,
Proud with his form, in his eye pride express'd;
His tongue, all impatient to speak and not see,
Did stumble with haste in his eyesight to be;
All senses to that sense did make their repair,
To feel only looking on fairest of fair.　　　　　240

Methought all his senses were lock'd in his eye,
As jewels in crystal for some prince to buy;
Who, tendering their own worth from where they were glass'd,
Did point you to buy them, along as you pass'd.
His face's own margent did quote such amazes
That all eyes saw his eyes enchanted with gazes.
I 'll give you Aquitaine and all that is his,
An you give him for my sake but one loving kiss.

   Princess. Come to our pavilion; Boyet is dispos'd.
   Boyet. But to speak that in words which his eye hath dis-
      clos'd.　　　　　　　　　　　　　　　　　　　　25''
I only have made a mouth of his eye,
By adding a tongue which I know will not lie.

   Rosaline. Thou art an old love-monger and speakest skil-
      fully.
   Maria. He is Cupid's grandfather and learns news of him.
   Rosaline. Then was Venus like her mother, for her father
      is but grim.
   Boyet. Do you hear, my mad wenches?
   Maria.　　　　　　　　　　　　　No.
   Boyet.　　　　　　　　　　　What then, do you see?
   Rosaline. Ay, our way to be gone.
   Boyet.　　　　　　　　　　You are too hard for me.
                         [*Exeunt.*

BIRON AND COSTARD (iii. 1. 165).

ACT III.

SCENE I. *The Park.*

Enter ARMADO *and* MOTH.

Armado. Warble, child; make passionate my sense of hearing.

MOTH *sings.—Concolinel.*

Armado. Sweet air!—Go, tenderness of years; take this key, give enlargement to the swain, bring him festinately hither. I must employ him in a letter to my love.

Moth. Master, will you win your love with a French brawl?

Armado. How meanest thou? brawling in French?

Moth. No, my complete master; but to jig off a tune at the tongue's end, canary to it with your feet, humour it with turning up your eye, sigh a note and sing a note, sometime through the throat, as if you swallowed love with singing love, sometime through the nose, as if you snuffed up love by smelling love; with your hat penthouse-like o'er the shop of your eyes; with your arms crossed on your thin-belly doublet like a rabbit on a spit, or your hands in your pocket like a man after the old painting; and keep not too long in one tune, but a snip and away. These are complements, these are humours; these betray nice wenches, that would be betrayed without these, and make them men of note—do you note me?—that most are affected to these. 21

Armado. How hast thou purchased this experience?

Moth. By my penny of observation.

Armado. But O,—but O,—

Moth. The hobby-horse is forgot.

Armado. Callest thou my love hobby-horse?

Moth. No, master; the hobby-horse is but a colt, and your love perhaps a hackney. But have you forgot your love?

Armado. Almost I had.

Moth. Negligent student! learn her by heart. 30

Armado. By heart and in heart, boy.

Moth. And out of heart, master; all those three I will prove.

Armado. What wilt thou prove?

Moth. A man, if I live; and this, by, in, and without, upon the instant: by heart you love her, because your heart cannot come by her; in heart you love her, because your heart is in love with her; and out of heart you love her, being out of heart that you cannot enjoy her.

Armado. I am all these three. 40

Moth. And three times as much more, and yet nothing at all.

Armado. Fetch hither the swain; he must carry me a letter.

Moth. A message well sympathized; a horse to be ambassador for an ass.

Armado. Ha, ha! what sayest thou?

Moth. Marry, sir, you must send the ass upon the horse, for he is very slow-gaited. But I go.

Armado. The way is but short; away! 50

Moth. As swift as lead, sir.

Armado. Thy meaning, pretty ingenious? Is not lead a metal heavy, dull, and slow?

Moth. Minime, honest master; or rather, master, no.

Armado. I say lead is slow.

Moth.   You are too swift, sir, to say so; Is that lead slow which is fir'd from a gun?

Armado. Sweet smoke of rhetoric! He reputes me a cannon; and the bullet, that 's he.— I shoot thee at the swain.

Moth.   Thump then, and I flee. [*Exit.*

Armado. A most acute juvenal; voluble and free of grace! By thy favour, sweet welkin, I must sigh in thy face.— 61 Most rude melancholy, valour gives thee place.— My herald is return'd.

Re-enter MOTH *with* COSTARD.

Moth. A wonder, master! here 's a costard broken in a shin.

Armado. Some enigma, some riddle: come, thy l'envoy; begin.

Costard. No egma, no riddle, no l'envoy; no salve in them all, sir. O, sir, plantain, a plain plantain! no l'envoy, no l'envoy; no salve, sir, but a plantain!

Armado. By virtue, thou enforcest laughter; thy silly thought my spleen; the heaving of my lungs provokes me to ridiculous smiling.—O, pardon me, my stars! Doth the inconsiderate take salve for l'envoy, and the word l'envoy for a salve? 73

Moth. Do the wise think them other? is not l'envoy a salve?

Armado. No, page; it is an epilogue or discourse, to make
    plain
Some obscure precedence that hath tofore been sain.
I will example it:
    The fox, the ape, and the humble-bee,
    Were still at odds, being but three.   80
There 's the moral.   Now the l'envoy.
  Moth. I will add the l'envoy.   Say the moral again.
  Armado. The fox, the ape, the humble-bee,
    Were still at odds, being but three.
  Moth.   Until the goose came out of door,
    And stay'd the odds by adding four.
Now will I begin your moral, and do you follow with my
l'envoy.
    The fox, the ape, and the humble-bee,
    Were still at odds, being but three.   90
  Armado. Until the goose came out of door,
    Staying the odds by adding four.
  Moth. A good l'envoy, ending in the goose; would you
desire more?
  Costard. The boy hath sold him a bargain, a goose, that 's
    flat.—
Sir, your pennyworth is good, an your goose be fat.—
To sell a bargain well is as cunning as fast and loose.
Let me see—a fat l'envoy; ay, that 's a fat goose.
  Armado. Come hither, come hither.   How did this argu-
    ment begin?
  Moth. By saying that a costard was broken in a shin.   100
Then call'd you for the l'envoy.
  Costard. True, and I for a plantain: thus came your ar-
    gument in;
Then the boy's fat l'envoy, the goose that you bought,
And he ended the market.
  Armado. But tell me; how was there a costard broken in
a shin?

Moth. I will tell you sensibly.

Costard. Thou hast no feeling of it, Moth; I will speak that l'envoy.

  I Costard, running out, that was safely within,   110
  Fell over the threshold, and broke my shin.

Armado. We will talk no more of this matter.

Costard. 'Till there be more matter in the shin.

Armado. Marry, Costard, I will enfranchise thee.

Costard. O, marry me to one Frances? I smell some l'envoy, some goose, in this.

Armado. By my sweet soul, I mean setting thee at liberty, enfreedoming thy person; thou wert immured, restrained, captivated, bound.

Costard. True, true; and now you will be my purgation and let me loose.   121

Armado. I give thee thy liberty, set thee from durance; and, in lieu thereof, impose on thee nothing but this: bear this significant [*giving a letter*] to the country maid Jaquenetta. There is remuneration; for the best ward of mine honour is rewarding my dependents.—Moth, follow. [*Exit.*

Moth. Like the sequel, I.—Signior Costard, adieu.

Costard. My sweet ounce of man's flesh! my incony Jew!
              [*Exit Moth.*

O' my troth, most sweet jests! most incony vulgar wit!
When it comes so smoothly off, so obscenely, as it were, so fit.
Armado o' th' one side,—O, a most dainty man!   131
To see him walk before a lady and to bear her fan!
To see him kiss his hand! and how most sweetly a' will
  swear!
And his page o' t' other side, that handful of wit!
Ah, heavens, it is a most pathetical nit!—
Now will I look to his remuneration. Remuneration! O, that 's the Latin word for three farthings; three farthings—remuneration. — 'What 's the price of this inkle?' — 'One penny.'—'No, I 'll give you a remuneration;' why, it carries

it. — Remuneration ! why, it is a fairer name than French
crown.   I will never buy and sell out of this word.   141

Enter BIRON.

Biron. O, my good knave Costard ! exceedingly well met.

Costard. Pray you, sir, how much carnation ribbon may a
man buy for a remuneration ?

Biron. What is a remuneration ?

Costard. Marry, sir, halfpenny farthing.

Biron. Why, then, three-farthing worth of silk.

Costard. I thank your worship ; God be wi' you !

Biron. Stay, slave !   I must employ thee ;
As thou wilt win my favour, good my knave,   150
Do one thing for me that I shall entreat.

Costard. When would you have it done, sir?

Biron. This afternoon.

Costard. Well, I will do it, sir ; fare you well.

Biron. Thou knowest not what it is.

Costard. I shall know, sir, when I have done it.

Biron. Why, villain, thou must know first.

Costard. I will come to your worship to-morrow morning.

Biron. It must be done this afternoon.   Hark, slave, it is
but this :   160
The princess comes to hunt here in the park,
And in her train there is a gentle lady ;
When tongues speak sweetly, then they name her name,
And Rosaline they call her : ask for her,
And to her white hand see thou do commend
This sealed-up counsel.   There 's thy guerdon ; go.
                              [*Giving him a shilling.*

Costard. Gardon. — O sweet gardon ! better than remuneration, a 'leven-pence farthing better : most sweet gardon ! — I
will do it, sir, in print. — Gardon !   Remuneration !   [*Exit.*

Biron. And I, forsooth, in love !   I that have been love's
whip ;   171

A very beadle to a humorous sigh;
A critic, nay, a night-watch constable ;
A domineering pedant o'er the boy,
Than whom no mortal so magnificent !
This wimpled, whining, purblind, wayward boy;
This senior-junior, giant-dwarf, Dan Cupid;
Regent of love-rhymes, lord of folded arms,
The anointed sovereign of sighs and groans,
Liege of all loiterers and malcontents,   180
Dread prince of plackets, king of codpieces,
Sole imperator and great general
Of trotting paritors,—O my little heart !—
And I to be a corporal of his field,
And wear his colours like a tumbler's hoop !
What, I ! I love ! I sue ! I seek a wife !
A woman, that is like a German clock,
Still a-repairing, ever out of frame,
And never going right, being a watch,
But being watch'd that it may still go right !   190
Nay, to be perjur'd, which is worst of all;
And, among three, to love the worst of all;
A wightly wanton with a velvet brow,
With two pitch-balls stuck in her face for eyes ;
Ay, and, by heaven, one that will do the deed,
Though Argus were her eunuch and her guard:
And I to sigh for her ! to watch for her !
To pray for her ! Go to ; it is a plague
That Cupid will impose for my neglect
Of his almighty dreadful little might.   200
Well, I will love, write, sigh, pray, sue, and groan ;
Some men must love my lady and some Joan.   [*Exit.*

E

ARMADO AND MOTH.

ACT IV.

Scene I. *The Park.*

Enter the Princess, *and her train, a* Forester, Boyet, Rosaline, Maria, *and* Katherine.

Princess. Was that the king, that spurr'd his horse so hard
Against the steep uprising of the hill?

Boyet. I know not; but I think it was not he.

Princess. Whoe'er he was, he show'd a mounting mind.
Well, lords, to-day we shall have our dispatch;
On Saturday we will return to France.—

Then, forester, my friend, where is the bush
That we must stand and play the murtherer in?
   Forester. Hereby, upon the edge of yonder coppice ;
A stand where you may make the fairest shoot.   10
   Princess. I thank my beauty, I am fair that shoot,
And thereupon thou speak'st the fairest shoot.
   Forester. Pardon me, madam, for I meant not so.
   Princess. What, what? first praise me and again say no?
O short-liv'd pride!   Not fair? alack for woe!
   Forester. Yes, madam, fair.
   Princess.   Nay, never paint me now ;
Where fair is not, praise cannot mend the brow.
Here, good my glass, take this for telling true ;
Fair payment for foul words is more than due.
   Forester. Nothing but fair is that which you inherit.   20
   Princess. See, see, my beauty will be sav'd by merit!
O heresy in fair, fit for these days!
A giving hand, though foul, shall have fair praise.—
But come, the bow ; now mercy goes to kill,
And shooting well is then accounted ill.
Thus will I save my credit in the shoot:
Not wounding, pity would not let me do 't ;
If wounding, then it was to show my skill,
That more for praise than purpose meant to kill.
And out of question so it is sometimes,   30
Glory grows guilty of detested crimes,
When, for fame's sake, for praise, an outward part,
We bend to that the working of the heart ;
As I for praise alone now seek to spill
The poor deer's blood, that my heart means no ill.
   Boyet. Do not curst wives hold that self-sovereignty
Only for praise sake, when they strive to be
Lords o'er their lords?
   Princess. Only for praise ; and praise we may afford
To any lady that subdues a lord.   40

Boyet. Here comes a member of the commonwealth.

Enter COSTARD.

Costard. God dig - you - den all!   Pray you, which is the
head lady?

Princess. Thou shalt know her, fellow, by the rest that
have no heads.

Costard. Which is the greatest lady, the highest?

Princess. The thickest and the tallest.

Costard. The thickest and the tallest! it is so ; truth is truth.
An your waist, mistress, were as slender as my wit,
One o' these maids' girdles for your waist should be fit.   50
Are not you the chief woman? you are the thickest here.

Princess. What 's your will, sir? what 's your will?

Costard. I have a letter from Monsieur Biron to one Lady
          Rosaline.

Princess. O, thy letter, thy letter! he 's a good friend of
          mine.
Stand aside, good bearer.—Boyet, you can carve ;
Break up this capon.

Boyet.   I am bound to serve.—
This letter is mistook, it importeth none here ;
It is writ to Jaquenetta.

Princess.   We will read it, I swear.
Break the neck of the wax, and every one give ear.   59

Boyet. [Reads] ' *By heaven, that thou art fair, is most infal-
lible ; true, that thou art beauteous ; truth itself, that thou art
lovely.   More fairer than fair, beautiful than beauteous, truer
than truth itself, have commiseration on thy heroical vassal!
The magnanimous and most illustrate king Cophetua set eye
upon the pernicious and indubitate beggar Zenelophon ; and he
it was that might rightly say, Veni, vidi, vici ; which to annothanize in the vulgar,—O base and obscure vulgar !—videlicet,
He came, saw, and overcame : he came, one ; saw, two ; overcame, three.   Who came ? the king : why did he come ? to see :*

*why did he see? to overcome: to whom came he? to the beggar:
what saw he? the beggar: who overcame he? the beggar. The
conclusion is victory: on whose side? the king's. The captive
is enriched: on whose side? the beggar's. The catastrophe is a
nuptial: on whose side? the king's: no, on both in one, or one
in both. I am the king; for so stands the comparison: thou
the beggar; for so witnesseth thy lowliness. Shall I command
thy love? I may: shall I enforce thy love? I could: shall I entreat thy love? I will. What shalt thou exchange for rags?
robes; for tittles? titles; for thyself? me. Thus, expecting thy
reply, I profane my lips on thy foot, my eyes on thy picture, and
my heart on thy every part. Thine, in the dearest design of in-
dustry,*   DON ADRIANO DE ARMADO.

  ' *Thus dost thou hear the Nemean lion roar*   83
     '*Gainst thee, thou lamb, that standest as his prey.*
  Submissive fall his princely feet before,
    And he from forage will incline to play;
  But if thou strive, poor soul, what art thou then?
  Food for his rage, repasture for his den.'

Princess. What plume of feathers is he that indited this
    letter?
What vane? what weathercock? did you ever hear better?
  Boyet. I am much deceiv'd but I remember the style.   91
  Princess. Else your memory is bad, going o'er it erewhile.
  Boyet. This Armado is a Spaniard, that keeps here in court;
A phantasime, a Monarcho, and one that makes sport
To the prince and his bookmates.
  Princess.   Thou fellow, a word:
Who gave thee this letter?
  Costard.   I told you; my lord.
  Princess. To whom shouldst thou give it?
  Costard.   From my lord to my lady.
  Princess. From which lord to which lady?
  Costard. From my lord Biron, a good master of mine,
To a lady of France that he called Rosaline.   100

Princess. Thou hast mistaken his letter. — Come, lords,
    away.

[*To Rosaline*] Here, sweet, put up this; 't will be thine an-
    other day.   [*Exeunt Princess and train.*

Boyet. Who is the suitor? who is the suitor?

Rosaline.   Shall I teach you to know?

Boyet. Ay, my continent of beauty.

Rosaline.   Why, she that bears the bow.

Finely put off!

Boyet. My lady goes to kill horns; but, if thou marry,
Hang me by the neck, if horns that year miscarry.

Finely put on!

Rosaline. Well, then, I am the shooter.

Boyet.   And who is your deer?

Rosaline. If we choose by the horns, yourself come not
    near.   110

Finely put on, indeed!

Maria. You still wrangle with her, Boyet, and she strikes
    at the brow.

Boyet. But she herself is hit lower. Have I hit her now?

Rosaline. Shall I come upon thee with an old saying, that
was a man when King Pepin of France was a little boy, as
touching the hit it?

Boyet. So I may answer thee with one as old, that was a
woman when Queen Guinever of Britain was a little wench,
as touching the hit it.

Rosaline.   *Thou canst not hit it, hit it, hit it,*   120
        Thou canst not hit it, my good man.

Boyet.   *An I cannot, cannot, cannot,*
        An I cannot, another can.

                [*Exit Rosaline and Katherine.*

Costard. By my troth, most pleasant! how both did fit
    it!

Maria. A mark marvellous well shot, for they both did
    hit it.

Boyet. A mark! O, mark but that mark! A mark, says
 my lady!
Let the mark have a prick in 't, to mete at, if it may be.
 Maria. Wide o' the bow hand! i' faith, your hand is out.
 Costard. Indeed, a' must shoot nearer, or he 'll ne'er hit
  the clout.   129
 Boyet. An if my hand be out, then belike your hand is in.
 Costard. Then will she get the upshoot by cleaving the pin.
 Maria. Come, come, you talk greasily; your lips grow foul.
 Costard. She 's too hard for you at pricks, sir; challenge
  her to bowl.
 Boyet. I fear too much rubbing. Good night, my good
  owl.   [*Exeunt Boyet and Maria.*
 Costard. By my soul, a swain! a most simple clown!
Lord, Lord, how the ladies and I have put him down!—
Sola, sola!   [*Shout within.*
         [*Exit Costard, running.*

SCENE II. *The Same.*

Enter HOLOFERNES, SIR NATHANIEL, *and* DULL.

Nathaniel. Very reverend sport, truly; and done in the
testimony of a good conscience.

Holofernes. The deer was, as you know, sanguis, in blood;
ripe as the pomewater, who now hangeth like a jewel in the
ear of caelo, the sky, the welkin, the heaven; and anon fall-
eth like a crab on the face of terra, the soil, the land, the
earth.

Nathaniel. Truly, Master Holofernes, the epithets are
sweetly varied, like a scholar at the least: but, sir, I assure
ye, it was a buck of the first head.   10

Holofernes. Sir Nathaniel, haud credo.

Dull. 'T was not a haud credo; 't was a pricket.

Holofernes. Most barbarous intimation! yet a kind of in-
sinuation, as it were, in via, in way, of explication; facere, as

it were, replication, or rather, ostentare, to show, as it were,
his inclination,—after his undressed, unpolished, uneducated,
unpruned, untrained, or rather, unlettered, or ratherest, unconfirmed fashion,—to insert again my haud credo for a
deer.   19

   Dull. I said the deer was not a haud credo; 't was a
     pricket.

   Holofernes. Twice-sod simplicity, bis coctus!—

O thou monster Ignorance, how deformed dost thou look!

   Nathaniel. Sir, he hath never fed of the dainties that are
     bred in a book;

he hath not eat paper, as it were; he hath not drunk ink:
his intellect is not replenished; he is only an animal, only
sensible in the duller parts:

And such barren plants are set before us, that we thankful
     should be,

Which we of taste and feeling are, for those parts that do
     fructify in us more than he.

For as it would ill become me to be vain, indiscreet, or a fool,

So were there a patch set on learning, to see him in a school:

But omne bene, say I; being of an old father's mind,   31

Many can brook the weather that love not the wind.

   Dull. You two are book-men: can you tell me by your wit

What was a month old at Cain's birth, that 's not five weeks
     old as yet?

   Holofernes. Dictynna, goodman Dull; Dictynna, goodman
     Dull.

   Dull. What is Dictynna?

   Nathaniel. A title to Phœbe, to Luna, to the moon.

   Holofernes. The moon was a month old when Adam was
     no more,

And raught not to five weeks when he came to five-score.

The allusion holds in the exchange.   40

   Dull. 'T is true indeed; the collusion holds in the ex-
     change.

Holofernes. God comfort thy capacity! I say, the allusion holds in the exchange.

Dull. And I say, the pollusion holds in the exchange; for the moon is never but a month old: and I say beside that, 't was a pricket that the princess killed.

Holofernes. Sir Nathaniel, will you hear an extemporal epitaph on the death of the deer? And, to humour the ignorant, call I the deer the princess killed a pricket.

Nathaniel. Perge, good Master Holofernes, perge; so it shall please you to abrogate scurrility. 51

Holofernes. I will something affect the letter, for it argues facility.

The preyful princess pierc'd and prick'd a pretty pleasing pricket;
Some say a sore; but not a sore, till now made sore with shooting.
The dogs did yell: put L to sore, then sorel jumps from thicket;
Or pricket sore, or else sorel; the people fall a-hooting.
If sore be sore, then L to sore makes fifty sores,—o sore L.
Of one sore I an hundred make by adding but one more L.

Nathaniel. A rare talent. 60

Dull. [*Aside*] If a talent be a claw, look how he claws him with a talent.

Holofernes. This is a gift that I have, simple, simple; a foolish extravagant spirit, full of forms, figures, shapes, objects, ideas, apprehensions, motions, revolutions: these are begot in the ventricle of memory, nourished in the womb of pia mater, and delivered upon the mellowing of occasion. But the gift is good in those in whom it is acute, and I am thankful for it. 69

Nathaniel. Sir, I praise the Lord for you: and so may my parishioners; for their sons are well tutored by you, and their daughters profit very greatly under you: you are a good member of the commonwealth.

Holofernes. Mehercle, if their sons be ingenuous, they shall want no instruction; if their daughters be capable, I will put it to them: but *vir sapit qui pauca loquitur*; a soul feminine saluteth us.

Enter JAQUENETTA *and* COSTARD.

Jaquenetta. God give you good morrow, master Person.

Holofernes. Master Person, quasi pers-on. An if one should be pierced, which is the one?　　　　　　80

Costard. Marry, master schoolmaster, he that is likest to a hogshead.

Holofernes. Piercing a hogshead! a good lustre of conceit in a tuft of earth; fire enough for a flint, pearl enough for a swine: 't is pretty; it is well.

Jaquenetta. Good master Person, be so good as read me this letter: it was given me by Costard, and sent me from Don Armado; I beseech you, read it.

Holofernes. Fauste, precor gelida quando pecus omne sub umbra Ruminat,—and so forth. Ah, good old Mantuan! I may speak of thee as the traveller doth of Venice;　　91

　　　　　Venetia, Venetia,
　　　　　Chi non ti vede non ti pretia.

Old Mantuan, old Mantuan! who understandeth thee not, loves thee not. Ut, re, sol, la, mi, fa. Under pardon, sir, what are the contents? or rather, as Horace says in his— What, my soul, verses?

Nathaniel. Ay, sir, and very learned.

Holofernes. Let me hear a staff, a stanza, a verse; lege, domine.　　　　　　100

Nathaniel. [Reads]

'*If love make me forsworn, how shall I swear to love?*
　Ah, never faith could hold, if not to beauty vow'd!
Though to myself forsworn, to thee I 'll faithful prove;
　Those thoughts to me were oaks, to thee like osiers
　　bow'd.

Study his bias leaves and makes his book thine eyes,
  Where all those pleasures live that art would comprehend;
If knowledge be the mark, to know thee shall suffice;
  Well learned is that tongue that well can thee commend,
All ignorant that soul that sees thee without wonder;
  Which is to me some praise that I thy parts admire.   110
Thy eye Jove's lightning bears, thy voice his dreadful thunder,
  Which, not to anger bent, is music and sweet fire.
Celestial as thou art, O, pardon love this wrong,
That sings heaven's praise with such an earthly tongue.'

Holofernes. You find not the apostrophas, and so miss the accent; let me supervise the canzonet.   Here are only numbers ratified; but, for the elegancy, facility, and golden cadence of poesy, caret.   Ovidius Naso was the man; and why, indeed, Naso, but for smelling out the odoriferous flowers of fancy, the jerks of invention?   Imitari is nothing; so doth the hound his master, the ape his keeper, the tired horse his rider.—But, damosella virgin, was this directed to you? 122

Jaquenetta. Ay, sir, from one Monsieur Biron, one of the strange queen's lords.

Holofernes. I will overglance the superscript: '*To the snow-white hand of the most beauteous Lady Rosaline.*'   I will look again on the intellect of the letter, for the nomination of the party writing to the person written unto: '*Your ladyship's in all desired employment, Biron.*'   Sir Nathaniel, this Biron is one of the votaries with the king; and here he hath framed a letter to a sequent of the stranger queen's, which accidentally, or by the way of progression, hath miscarried.—Trip and go, my sweet; deliver this paper into the royal hand of the king: it may concern much.   Stay not thy compliment; I forgive thy duty: adieu.

Jaquenetta. Good Costard, go with me.—Sir, God save your life!

Costard. Have with thee, my girl.

                    [*Exeunt Costard and Jaquenetta.*

Nathaniel. Sir, you have done this in the fear of God, very religiously; and, as a certain father saith,—   140

Holofernes. Sir, tell not me of the father; I do fear colourable colours. But to return to the verses: did they please you, Sir Nathaniel?

Nathaniel. Marvellous well for the pen.

Holofernes. I do dine to day at the father's of a certain pupil of mine; where, if, before repast, it shall please you to gratify the table with a grace, I will, on my privilege 1 have with the parents of the foresaid child or pupil, undertake your ben venuto; where I will prove those verses to be very unlearned, neither savouring of poetry, wit, nor invention. I beseech your society.   151

Nathaniel. And thank you too; for society, saith the text, is the happiness of life.

Holofernes. And, certes, the text most infallibly concludes it.—[*To Dull*] Sir, I do invite you too; you shall not say me nay; pauca verba. Away! the gentles are at their game, and we will to our recreation.   [*Exeunt.*

SCENE III. *The Same.*

Enter BIRON, *with a paper.*

Biron. The king he is hunting the deer; I am coursing myself: they have pitched a toil; I am toiling in a pitch,— pitch that defiles. Defile! a foul word. Well, set thee down, sorrow! for so they say the fool said, and so say I, and ay the fool. Well proved, wit! By the Lord, this love is as mad as Ajax: it kills sheep; it kills me, ay, a sheep. Well proved again o' my side! I will not love: if I do, hang me; i' faith, I will not. O, but her eye,—by this light, but for her eye, I would not love her; yes, for her two eyes. Well, I do nothing in the world but lie, and lie in my throat. By heaven, I do love: and it hath taught me to rhyme and to be melancholy; and here is part of my rhyme, and here my melancholy. Well, she hath one o' my sonnets already: the clown bore it, the fool sent it, and the lady hath it; sweet clown, sweeter fool, sweetest lady! By the world, I would not care a pin, if the other three were in.—Here comes one with a paper; God give him grace to groan! [*Gets up into a tree.*

Enter the KING, *with a paper.*

King. Ay me!
Biron. [*Aside*] Shot, by heaven!—Proceed, sweet Cupid; thou hast thumped him with thy bird-bolt under the left pap.—In faith, secrets! 21
King. [Reads]

> *So sweet a kiss the golden sun gives not*
>> *To those fresh morning drops upon the rose,*
> *As thy eye-beams, when their fresh rays have smote*
>> *The night of dew that on my cheeks down flows:*
> *Nor shines the silver moon one half so bright*
>> *Through the transparent bosom of the deep,*
> *As doth thy face through tears of mine give light;*
>> *Thou shin'st in every tear that I do weep:*
> *No drop but as a coach doth carry thee;* 30
>> *So ridest thou triumphing in my woe.*
> *Do but behold the tears that swell in me,*
>> *And they thy glory through my grief will show:*
> *But do not love thyself; then thou wilt keep*
> *My tears for glasses, and still make me weep.*
> *O queen of queens! how far dost thou excel,*
> *No thought can think, nor tongue of mortal tell.*

How shall she know my griefs? I'll drop the paper.
Sweet leaves, shade folly.—Who is he comes here?
[*Steps aside.*
What, Longaville! and reading! listen, ear. 40
Biron. Now, in thy likeness, one more fool appear!

Enter LONGAVILLE, *with a paper.*

Longaville. Ay me, I am forsworn!

Biron. Why, he comes in like a perjure, wearing papers.

King. In love, I hope; sweet fellowship in shame!

Biron. One drunkard loves another of the name.

Longaville. Am I the first that have been perjur'd so?

Biron. I could put thee in comfort,—not by two that I know.
Thou mak'st the triumviry, the corner-cap of society,
The shape of Love's Tyburn that hangs up simplicity.

Longaville. I fear these stubborn lines lack power to move.—
O sweet Maria, empress of my love!—   51
These numbers will I tear, and write in prose.

Biron. O, rhymes are guards on wanton Cupid's hose;
Disfigure not his slop.

Longaville.   This same shall go.—
[*Reads*] *Did not the heavenly rhetoric of thine eye,*
   'Gainst whom the world cannot hold argument,
Persuade my heart to this false perjury?
   Vows for thee broke deserve not punishment.
A woman I forswore; but I will prove,
   Thou being a goddess, I forswore not thee: 60
My vow was earthly, thou a heavenly love;
   Thy grace being gain'd cures all disgrace in me.
Vows are but breath, and breath a vapour is:
   Then thou, fair sun, which on my earth dost shine,
Exhal'st this vapour-vow; in thee it is.
   If broken then, it is no fault of mine;
If by me broke, what fool is not so wise
   To lose an oath to win a paradise?

Biron. This is the liver-vein, which makes flesh a deity,
A green goose a goddess; pure, pure idolatry.   70
God amend us, God amend! we are much out o' the way.

Longaville. By whom shall I send this?—Company! stay.
                              [*Steps aside.*

Biron. All hid, all hid; an old infant play.
Like a demigod here sit I in the sky,
And wretched fools' secrets heedfully o'er-eye.—
More sacks to the mill! O heavens, I have my wish!

Enter DUMAIN, *with a paper.*

Dumain transform'd! four woodcocks in a dish!
  Dumain. O most divine Kate!
  Biron. O most profane coxcomb!
  Dumain. By heaven, the wonder in a mortal eye!   80
  Biron. By earth, she is not, corporal, there you lie.
  Dumain. Her amber hairs for foul hath amber quoted.
  Biron. An amber-colour'd raven was well noted.
  Dumain. As upright as the cedar.
  Biron.   Stoop, I say;
Her shoulder is with child.
  Dumain.   As fair as day.
  Biron. Ay, as some days; but then no sun must shine.
  Dumain. O that I had my wish!
  Longaville.   And I had mine!
  King. And I mine too, good Lord!
  Biron. Amen, so I had mine: is not that a good word?
  Dumain. I would forget her; but a fever she   90
Reigns in my blood and will remember'd be.
  Biron. A fever in your blood! why, then incision
Would let her out in saucers; sweet misprision!
  Dumain. Once more I'll read the ode that I have writ.
  Biron. Once more I'll mark how love can vary wit.
  Dumain. [Reads]

        On a day—alack the day!—
        Love, whose month is ever May,
        Spied a blossom passing fair
        Playing in the wanton air;
        Through the velvet leaves the wind,   100
        All unseen can passage find;

> *That the lover, sick to death,*
> *Wish'd himself the heaven's breath.*
> *Air, quoth he, thy cheeks may blow;*
> *Air, would I might triumph so!*
> *But, alack, my hand is sworn*
> *Ne'er to pluck thee from thy thorn;*
> *Vow, alack, for youth unmeet,*
> *Youth so apt to pluck a sweet!*
> *Do not call it sin in me,*   110
> *That I am forsworn for thee;*
> *Thou for whom Jove would swear*
> *Juno but an Ethiope were,*
> *And deny himself for Jove,*
> *Turning mortal for thy love.*

This will I send and something else more plain,
That shall express my true love's fasting pain.
O, would the king, Biron, and Longaville,
Were lovers too!   Ill, to example ill,
Would from my forehead wipe a perjur'd note;   120
For none offend where all alike do dote.

   Longaville. [*Advancing*] Dumain, thy love is far from charity,
That in love's grief desir'st society;
You may look pale, but I should blush, I know,
To be o'erheard and taken napping so.

   King. [*Advancing*] Come, sir, you blush; as his your case
      is such;
You chide at him, offending twice as much;
You do not love Maria; Longaville
Did never sonnet for her sake compile,
Nor never lay his wreathed arms athwart   130
His loving bosom to keep down his heart.
I have been closely shrouded in this bush
And mark'd you both, and for you both did blush.
I heard your guilty rhymes, observ'd your fashion,
Saw sighs reek from you, noted well your passion:

Ay me, says one ; O Jove ! the other cries ;
One, her hairs were gold, crystal the other's eyes.—
[*To Longaville*] You would for paradise break faith and
    troth ;—
[*To Dumain*] And Jove, for your love, would infringe an oath.
What will Biron say when that he shall hear   140
Faith so infringed, which such zeal did swear?
How will he scorn! how will he spend his wit!
How will he triumph, leap, and laugh at it!
For all the wealth that ever I did see,
I would not have him know so much by me.
    Biron. Now step I forth to whip hypocrisy.— [*Advancing.*
Ah, good my liege, I pray thee, pardon me !
Good heart, what grace hast thou, thus to reprove
These worms for loving, that art most in love?
Your eyes do make no coaches ; in your tears   150
There is no certain princess that appears ;
You 'll not be perjur'd, 't is a hateful thing ;
Tush, none but minstrels like of sonneting !
But are you not asham'd? nay, are you not,
All three of you, to be thus much o'ershot?
You found his mote ; the king your mote did see ;
But I a beam do find in each of three.
O, what a scene of foolery have I seen,
Of sighs, of groans, of sorrow, and of teen !
O me, with what strict patience have I sat,   160
To see a king transformed to a gnat !
To see great Hercules whipping a gig,
And profound Solomon to tune a jig,
And Nestor play at push-pin with the boys,
And critic Timon laugh at idle toys !
Where lies thy grief, O, tell me, good Dumain?—
And, gentle Longaville, where lies thy pain?—
And where my liege's ? all about the breast.—
A caudle, ho !

King.   Too bitter is thy jest.
Are we betray'd thus to thy over-view?   170
  Biron. Not you to me, but I betray'd by you :
I, that am honest; I, that hold it sin
To break the vow I am engaged in ;
I am betray'd, by keeping company
With men like you, men of inconstancy.
When shall you see me write a thing in rhyme?
Or groan for love? or spend a minute's time
In pruning me? When shall you hear that I
Will praise a hand, a foot, a face, an eye,
A gait, a state, a brow, a breast, a waist,   180
A leg, a limb?—
  King.   Soft! whither away so fast?
A true man or a thief that gallops so?
  Biron. I post from love ; good lover, let me go.

Enter JAQUENETTA *and* COSTARD.

Jaquenetta. God bless the king!
King.   What present hast thou there?
Costard. Some certain treason.
King.   What makes treason here?
Costard. Nay, it makes nothing, sir.
King.   If it mar nothing neither,
The treason and you go in peace away together.
  Jaquenetta. I beseech your grace let this letter be read:
Our person misdoubts it; 't was treason, he said.
  King. Biron, read it over.—   [*Giving him the paper.*
Where hadst thou it?   191
  Jaquenetta. Of Costard.
King. Where hadst thou it?
Costard. Of Dun Adramadio, Dun Adramadio.
                    [*Biron tears the letter.*
King. How now! what is in you? why dost thou tear it?
Biron. A toy, my liege, a toy; your grace needs not fear it.

Longaville. It did move him to passion, and therefore let 's
    hear it.

Dumain. It is Biron's writing, and here is his name.
                         [*Gathering up the pieces.*

Biron. [*To Costard*] Ah, you whoreson loggerhead! you
    were born to do me shame.—

Guilty, my lord, guilty! I confess, I confess.   200

    King. What?

    Biron. That you three fools lack'd me fool to make up the
    mess.

He, he, and you, and you, my liege, and I,

Are pick-purses in love, and we deserve to die.

O, dismiss this audience, and I shall tell you more.

    Dumain. Now the number is even.

    Biron.   True, true ; we are four.—

Will these turtles be gone?

    King.   Hence, sirs ; away!

    Costard. Walk aside the true folk, and let the traitors stay.
                  [*Exeunt Costard and Jaquenetta.*

    Biron. Sweet lords, sweet lovers, O, let us embrace !

As true we are as flesh and blood can be :   210

The sea will ebb and flow, heaven show his face ;

    Young blood doth not obey an old decree.

We cannot cross the cause why we were born ;

Therefore of all hands must we be forsworn.

    King. What, did these rent lines show some love of thine?

    Biron. Did they, quoth you? Who sees the heavenly Ros-
    aline,

That, like a rude and savage man of Inde,

    At the first opening of the gorgeous east,

Bows not his vassal head, and strucken blind

    Kisses the base ground with obedient breast?   220

What peremptory eagle-sighted eye

    Dares look upon the heaven of her brow,

That is not blinded by her majesty?

King. What zeal, what fury hath inspir'd thee now?
My love, her mistress, is a gracious moon;
   She an attending star, scarce seen a light.
Biron. My eyes are then no eyes, nor I Biron.
   O, but for my love, day would turn to night!
Of all complexions the cull'd sovereignty
   Do meet, as at a fair, in her fair cheek,   230
Where several worthies make one dignity,
   Where nothing wants that want itself doth seek.
Lend me the flourish of all gentle tongues,—
   Fie, painted rhetoric! O, she needs it not:
To things of sale a seller's praise belongs,
   She passes praise; then praise too short doth blot.
A wither'd hermit, five-score winters worn,
   Might shake off fifty, looking in her eye;
Beauty doth varnish age, as if new-born,
   And gives the crutch the cradle's infancy.   240
O, 't is the sun that maketh all things shine.
   King. By heaven, thy love is black as ebony.
Biron. Is ebony like her? O wood divine!
   A wife of such wood were felicity.
O, who can give an oath? where is a book?
   That I may swear beauty doth beauty lack,
If that she learn not of her eye to look;
   No face is fair that is not full so black.
King. O paradox! Black is the badge of hell,
   The hue of dungeons, and the shade of night;   250
And beauty's crest becomes the heavens well.
   Biron. Devils soonest tempt, resembling spirits of light.
O, if in black my lady's brows be deck'd,
   It mourns that painting and usurping hair
Should ravish doters with a false aspect;
   And therefore is she born to make black fair.
Her favour turns the fashion of the days;
   For native blood is counted painting now,

And therefore red, that would avoid dispraise,
   Paints itself black, to imitate her brow.   260

Dumain. To look like her are chimney-sweepers black.

   Longaville. And since her time are colliers counted bright.

King. And Ethiopes of their sweet complexion crack.

   Dumain. Dark needs no candles now, for dark is light.

Biron. Your mistresses dare never come in rain,
   For fear their colours should be wash'd away.

King. 'T were good, yours did ; for, sir, to tell you plain,
   I 'll find a fairer face not wash'd to-day.

Biron. I 'll prove her fair, or talk till doomsday here.

   King. No devil will fright thee then so much as she.   270

Dumain. I never knew man hold vile stuff so dear.

   Longaville. Look, here 's thy love ; my foot and her face
     see.

Biron. O, if the streets were paved with thine eyes,
   Her feet were much too dainty for such tread !

Dumain. O vile ! then, as she goes, what upward lies
   The street should see as she walk'd overhead.

King. But what of this ? are we not all in love ?

   Biron. Nothing so sure ; and thereby all forsworn.

King. Then leave this chat ; and, good Biron, now prove
   Our loving lawful, and our faith not torn.   280

Dumain. Ay, marry, there ; some flattery for this evil.

   Longaville. O, some authority how to proceed ;
Some tricks, some quillets, how to cheat the devil.

   Dumain. Some salve for perjury.

   Biron.   'T is more than need.
Have at you, then, affection's men at arms.
Consider what you first did swear unto,—
To fast, to study, and to see no woman ;
Flat treason 'gainst the kingly state of youth.
Say, can you fast ? your stomachs are too young,
And abstinence engenders maladies.   290
And where that you have vow'd to study, lords,

In that each of you have forsworn his book,
Can you still dream and pore and thereon look?
[For when would you, my lord,—or you,—or you,—
Have found the ground of study's excellence
Without the beauty of a woman's face?
From women's eyes this doctrine I derive:
They are the ground, the books, the academes,
From whence doth spring the true Promethean fire.]
Why, universal plodding poisons up   300
The nimble spirits in the arteries,
As motion and long-during action tires
The sinewy vigour of the traveller.
Now, for not looking on a woman's face,
You have in that forsworn the use of eyes,
And study too, the causer of your vows;
[For where is any author in the world
Teaches such beauty as a woman's eye?
Learning is but an adjunct to ourself,
And where we are our learning likewise is;   310
Then when ourselves we see in ladies' eyes,
Do we not likewise see our learning there?
O, we have made a vow to study, lords,
And in that vow we have forsworn our books.]
For when would you, my liege,—or you,—or you,—
In leaden contemplation have found out
Such fiery numbers as the prompting eyes
Of beauty's tutors have enrich'd you with?
Other slow arts entirely keep the brain,
And therefore, finding barren practisers,   320
Scarce show a harvest of their heavy toil;
But love, first learned in a lady's eyes,
Lives not alone immured in the brain,
But, with the motion of all elements,
Courses as swift as thought in every power,
And gives to every power a double power,

Above their functions and their offices.
It adds a precious seeing to the eye ;
A lover's eyes will gaze an eagle blind ;
A lover's ear will hear the lowest sound,   330
When the suspicious head of theft is stopp'd ;
Love's feeling is more soft and sensible
Than are the tender horns of cockled snails ;
Love's tongue proves dainty Bacchus gross in taste ;
For valour, is not Love a Hercules,
Still climbing trees in the Hesperides ?
Subtle as Sphinx ; as sweet and musical
As bright Apollo's lute, strung with his hair ;
And when Love speaks, the voice of all the gods
Make heaven drowsy with the harmony.   340
Never durst poet touch a pen to write
Until his ink were temper'd with Love's sighs ;
O, then his lines would ravish savage ears
And plant in tyrants mild humility !
From women's eyes this doctrine I derive :
They sparkle still the right Promethean fire ;
They are the books, the arts, the academes,
That show, contain, and nourish all the world,
Else none at all in aught proves excellent.
Then fools you were these women to forswear,   350
Or keeping what is sworn, you will prove fools.
For wisdom's sake, a word that all men love,
Or for love's sake, a word that loves all men,
Or for men's sake, the authors of these women,
Or women's sake, by whom we men are men,
Let us once lose our oaths to find ourselves,
Or else we lose ourselves to keep our oaths.
It is religion to be thus forsworn,
For charity itself fulfils the law,—
And who can sever love from charity ?   360
    King. Saint Cupid, then ! and, soldiers, to the field !

Biron. Advance your standards, and upon them, lords!
Pell-mell, down with them! but be first advis'd,
In conflict that you get the sun of them.

Longaville. Now to plain-dealing; lay these glozes by:
Shall we resolve to woo these girls of France?

King. And win them too; therefore let us devise
Some entertainment for them in their tents.

Biron. First, from the park let us conduct them thither;
Then homeward every man attach the hand   370
Of his fair mistress.   In the afternoon
We will with some strange pastime solace them,
Such as the shortness of the time can shape;
For revels, dances, masks, and merry hours
Forerun fair Love, strewing her way with flowers.

King. Away, away! no time shall be omitted
That will be time, and may by us be fitted.

Biron. Allons! allons!—Sow'd cockle reap'd no corn;
And justice always whirls in equal measure;
Light wenches may prove plagues to men forsworn;   380
If so, our copper buys no better treasure.   [*Exeunt.*

CUPID WHETTING HIS DARTS.   FROM AN ANTIQUE GEM.

HOLOFERNES AND MOTH (V. 2. 583).

ACT V.

SCENE I. *The Park.*

Enter HOLOFERNES, SIR NATHANIEL, *and* DULL.

Holofernes. Satis quod sufficit.

Nathaniel. I praise God for you, sir: your reasons at dinner have been sharp and sententious; pleasant without scurrility, witty without affection, audacious without impudency, learned without opinion, and strange without heresy. I did converse this quondam day with a companion of the king's, who is intituled, nominated, or called, Don Adriano de Armado.

Holofernes. Novi hominem tanquam te; his humour is lofty, his discourse peremptory, his tongue filed, his eye ambitious, his gait majestical, and his general behaviour vain, ridiculous, and thrasonical. He is too picked, too spruce, too affected, too odd, as it were, too peregrinate, as I may call it.

Nathaniel. A most singular and choice epithet.   15
                                  [*Draws out his table-book.*

Holofernes. He draweth out the thread of his verbosity finer than the staple of his argument. I abhor such fanatical phantasimes, such insociable and point-device companions; such rackers of orthography, as to speak dout, fine, when he should say doubt; det, when he should pronounce debt,—d, e, b, t, not d, e, t; he clepeth a calf, cauf; half, hauf; neighbour vocatur nebour; neigh abbreviated ne. This is abhominable,—which he would call abominable: it insinuateth me of insanire: ne intelligis, domine? to make frantic, lunatic.

Nathaniel. Laus Deo, bone, intelligo.

Holofernes. Bone!—bone for bene! Priscian a little scratched; 't will serve.

Nathaniel. Videsne quis venit?

Holofernes. Video, et gaudeo.   30

Enter ARMADO, MOTH, *and* COSTARD.

Armado. Chirrah!   [*To Moth.*

Holofernes. Quare chirrah, not sirrah?

Armado. Men of peace, well encountered.

Holofernes. Most military sir, salutation.

Moth. [*Aside to Costard*] They have been at a great feast of languages, and stolen the scraps.

Costard. O, they have lived long on the alms-basket of
words.   I marvel thy master hath not eaten thee for a word;
for thou art not so long by the head as honorificabilitudinitatibus: thou art easier swallowed than a flap-dragon.   40

Moth. Peace! the peal begins.

Armado. [*To Holofernes*] Monsieur, are you not lettered?

Moth. Yes, yes; he teaches boys the horn-book.   What is
a, b, spelt backward, with the horn on his head?

Holofernes. Ba, pueritia, with a horn added.

Moth. Ba, most silly sheep with a horn!   You hear his
learning.

Holofernes. Quis, quis, thou consonant?

Moth. The third of the five vowels, if you repeat them;
or the fifth, if I.   50

Holofernes. I will repeat them,—a, e, i,—

Moth. The sheep; the other two concludes it,—o, u.

Armado. Now, by the salt wave of the Mediterraneum, a
sweet touch, a quick venue of wit! snip, snap, quick and
home! it rejoiceth my intellect; true wit!

Moth. Offered by a child to an old man; which is wit-old.

Holofernes. What is the figure? what is the figure?

Moth. Horns.

Holofernes. Thou disputest like an infant; go, whip thy
gig.   60

Moth. Lend me your horn to make one, and I will whip
about your infamy circum circa,—a gig of a cuckold's horn.

Costard. An I had but one penny in the world, thou shouldst
have it to buy gingerbread.   Hold, there is the very remuneration I had of thy master, thou halfpenny purse of wit,
thou pigeon-egg of discretion.   O, an the heavens were so
pleased that thou wert but my bastard, what a joyful father
wouldst thou make me!   Go to; thou hast it ad dunghill, at
the finger's ends, as they say.   69

Holofernes. O, I smell false Latin; dunghill for unguem.

Armado. Arts-man, preambulate; we will be singled from

the barbarous. Do you not educate youth at the charge
house on the top of the mountain?

Holofernes. Or mons, the hill.

Armado. At your sweet pleasure, for the mountain.

Holofernes. I do, sans question.

Armado. Sir, it is the king's most sweet pleasure and affection to congratulate the princess at her pavilion in the posteriors of this day, which the rude multitude call the afternoon.   80

Holofernes. The posterior of the day, most generous sir, is
liable, congruent, and measurable for the afternoon; the word
is well culled, choice, sweet, and apt, I do assure you, sir, I
do assure.

Armado. Sir, the king is a noble gentleman, and my familiar, I do assure ye, very good friend; for what is inward between us, let it pass. I do beseech thee, remember thy
courtesy,—I beseech thee, apparel thy head;—and among
other importunate and most serious designs, and of great
import indeed, too,—but let that pass:—for I must tell thee,
it will please his grace, by the world, sometime to lean upon
my poor shoulder, and with his royal finger, thus, dally with
my excrement, with my mustachio;—but, sweet heart, let
that pass. By the world, I recount no fable: some certain
special honours it pleaseth his greatness to impart to Armado, a soldier, a man of travel, that hath seen the world;—
but let that pass.—The very all of all is,—but, sweet heart, I
do implore secrecy,—that the king would have me present
the princess, sweet chuck, with some delightful ostentation,
or show, or pageant, or antique, or firework. Now, understanding that the curate and your sweet self are good at
such eruptions and sudden breaking out of mirth, as it were,
I have acquainted you withal, to the end to crave your as-
sistance.   104

Holofernes. Sir, you shall present before her the Nine Worthies.—Sir Nathaniel, as concerning some entertainment of

time, some show in the posterior of this day, to be rendered
by our assistants, at the king's command, and this most gallant, illustrate, and learned gentleman, before the princess,—
I say none so fit as to present the Nine Worthies.   110

Nathaniel. Where will you find men worthy enough to present them?

Holofernes. Joshua, yourself; myself or this gallant gentleman, Judas Maccabæus; this swain, because of his great
limb or joint, shall pass Pompey the Great; the page, Hercules,—

Armado. Pardon, sir; error: he is not quantity enough
for that Worthy's thumb; he is not so big as the end of his
club.   119

Holofernes. Shall I have audience? he shall present Hercules in minority: his enter and exit shall be strangling a
snake; and I will have an apology for that purpose.

Moth. An excellent device! so, if any of the audience hiss,
you may cry 'Well done, Hercules! now thou crushest the
snake!' that is the way to make an offence gracious, though
few have the grace to do it.

Armado. For the rest of the Worthies?—

Holofernes. I will play three myself.

Moth. Thrice worthy gentleman!

Armado. Shall I tell you a thing?   130

Holofernes. We attend.

Armado. We will have, if this fadge not, an antique. I
beseech you, follow.

Holofernes. Via!—Goodman Dull, thou hast spoken no
word all this while.

Dull. Nor understood none neither, sir.

Holofernes. Allons! we will employ thee.

Dull. I'll make one in a dance, or so; or I will play
On the tabor to the Worthies, and let them dance the hay.

Holofernes. Most dull, honest Dull!—To our sport, away!
                                        [*Exeunt.*

SCENE II.   *The Same.*

Enter the PRINCESS, KATHERINE, ROSALINE, *and* MARIA.

Princess. Sweet hearts, we shall be rich ere we depart,
If fairings come thus plentifully in.
A lady wall'd about with diamonds !—
Look you what I have from the loving king.

Rosaline. Madame, came nothing else along with that?

Princess. Nothing but this! yes, as much love in rhyme
As would be cramm'd up in a sheet of paper,
Writ on both sides the leaf, margent and all,
That he was fain to seal on Cupid's name.

Rosaline. That was the way to make his godhead wax,   10
For he hath been five thousand years a boy.

Katherine. Ay, and a shrewd, unhappy gallows too.

Rosaline. You 'll ne'er be friends with him ; he kill'd your
        sister.

Katherine. He made her melancholy, sad, and heavy ;
And so she died.   Had she been light, like you,
Of such a merry, nimble, stirring spirit,
She might ha' been a grandam ere she died ;
And so may you, for a light heart lives long.

Rosaline. What 's your dark meaning, mouse, of this light
        word?

Katherine. A light condition in a beauty dark.   20

Rosaline. We need more light to find your meaning out.

Katherine. You 'll mar the light by taking it in snuff ;
Therefore I 'll darkly end the argument.

Rosaline. Look, what you do, you do it still i' the dark.

Katherine. So do not you, for you are a light wench.

Rosaline. Indeed I weigh not you, and therefore light.

Katherine. You weigh me not?   O, that 's you care not for
        me.

Rosaline. Great reason ; for past cure is still past care.

Princess. Well bandied both ; a set of wit well play'd.—

But, Rosaline, you have a favour, too.   30
Who sent it? and what is it?
 Rosaline.   I would you knew.
An if my face were but as fair as yours,
My favour were as great; be witness this.
Nay, I have verses too, I thank Biron:
The numbers true; and, were the numbering too,
I were the fairest goddess on the ground.
I am compar'd to twenty thousand fairs.
O, he hath drawn my picture in his letter!
 Princess. Any thing like?
 Rosaline. Much in the letters, nothing in the praise.   40
 Princess. Beauteous as ink; a good conclusion.
 Katherine. Fair as a text B in a copy-book.
 Rosaline. Ware pencils, ho! let me not die your debtor,
My red dominical, my golden letter!
O that your face were not so full of O's!
 Katherine. A pox of that jest! and beshrew all shrows.
 Princess. But, Katherine, what was sent to you from fair
  Dumain?
 Katherine. Madam, this glove.
 Princess.   Did he not send you twain?
 Katherine. Yes, madam, and moreover
Some thousand verses of a faithful lover,—   50
A huge translation of hypocrisy,
Vilely compil'd, profound simplicity.
 Maria. This and these pearls to me sent Longaville;
The letter is too long by half a mile.
 Princess. I think no less. Dost thou not wish in heart
The chain were longer and the letter short?
 Maria. Ay, or I would these hands might never part.
 Princess. We are wise girls to mock our lovers so.
 Rosaline. They are worse fools to purchase mocking
  so.
That same Biron I 'll torture ere I go.   60

O that I knew he were but in by the week!
How I would make him fawn and beg and seek,
And wait the season, and observe the times,
And spend his prodigal wits in bootless rhymes,
And shape his service wholly to my hests,
And make him proud to make me proud that jests!
So potent-like would I o'ersway his state
That he should be my fool and I his fate.

    Princess. None are so surely caught, when they are catch'd,
As wit turn'd fool; folly, in wisdom hatch'd,   70
Hath wisdom's warrant and the help of school,
And wit's own grace to grace a learned fool.

    Rosaline. The blood of youth burns not with such excess
As gravity's revolt to wantonness.

    Maria. Folly in fools bears not so strong a note
As foolery in the wise, when wit doth dote;
Since all the power thereof it doth apply
To prove, by wit, worth in simplicity.

    Princess. Here comes Boyet, and mirth is in his face.   79

Enter BOYET.

    Boyet. O, I am stabb'd with laughter! Where's her grace?
    Princess. Thy news, Boyet?
    Boyet.   Prepare, madam, prepare!—
Arm, wenches, arm! encounters mounted are
Against your peace. Love doth approach disguis'd,
Armed in arguments; you 'll be surpris'd.
Muster your wits, stand in your own defence;
Or hide your heads like cowards, and fly hence.

    Princess. Saint Denis to Saint Cupid! What are they
That charge their breath against us? say, scout, say.

    Boyet. Under the cool shade of a sycamore
I thought to close mine eyes some half an hour,   90
When, lo! to interrupt my purpos'd rest,
Toward that shade I might behold addrest

The king and his companions ; warily
I stole into a neighbour thicket by,
And overheard what you shall overhear,—
That, by and by, disguis'd they will be here.
Their herald is a pretty knavish page,
That well by heart hath conn'd his embassage.
Action and accent did they teach him there,—
'Thus must thou speak,' and 'thus thy body bear ;' 100
And ever and anon they made a doubt
Presence majestical would put him out :
'For,' quoth the king, 'an angel shalt thou see ;
Yet fear not thou, but speak audaciously.'
The boy replied, 'An angel is not evil ;
I should have fear'd her had she been a devil.'
With that, all laugh'd and clapp'd him on the shoulder,
Making the bold wag by their praises bolder.
One rubb'd his elbow thus, and fleer'd, and swore
A better speech was never spoke before ; 110
Another, with his finger and his thumb,
Cried, 'Via ! we will do 't, come what will come ;'
The third he caper'd, and cried, 'All goes well ;'
The fourth turn'd on the toe, and down he fell.
With that, they all did tumble on the ground,
With such a zealous laughter, so profound,
That in this spleen ridiculous appears,
To check their folly, passion's solemn tears.
    Princess. But what, but what, come they to visit us ?
    Boyet. They do, they do ; and are apparell'd thus, 120
Like Muscovites or Russians, as I guess.
Their purpose is to parle, to court, and dance ;
And every one his love-feat will advance
Unto his several mistress, which they 'll know
By favours several which they did bestow.
    Princess. And will they so ? the gallants shall be task'd ;
For, ladies, we will every one be mask'd,

G

And not a man of them shall have the grace,
Despite of suit, to see a lady's face.—
Hold, Rosaline, this favour thou shalt wear,   130
And then the king will court thee for his dear ;
Hold, take thou this, my sweet, and give me thine,
So shall Biron take me for Rosaline.—
And change you favours too ; so shall your loves
Woo contrary, deceiv'd by these removes.

 Rosaline. Come on, then ; wear the favours most in sight.
 Katherine. But in this changing what is your intent?
 Princess. The effect of my intent is to cross theirs ;
They do it but in mocking merriment,
And mock for mock is only my intent.   140
Their several counsels they unbosom shall
To loves mistook, and so be mock'd withal
Upon the next occasion that we meet,
With visages display'd, to talk and greet.

 Rosaline. But shall we dance, if they desire us to 't?
 Princess. No, to the death, we will not move a foot ;
Nor to their penn'd speech render we no grace,
But while 't is spoke each turn away her face.

 Boyet. Why, that contempt will kill the speaker's heart,
And quite divorce his memory from his part.   150
 Princess. Therefore I do it ; and I make no doubt
The rest will ne'er come in, if he be out.
There 's no such sport as sport by sport o'erthrown,
To make theirs ours, and ours none but our own ;
So shall we stay, mocking intended game,
And they, well mock'd, depart away with shame.

        [*Trumpets sound within.*
 Boyet. The trumpet sounds : be mask'd ; the maskers
  come.   [*The Ladies mask.*

Enter Blackamoors with music; MOTH; *the* KING, BIRON,
LONGAVILLE, *and* DUMAIN, *in Russian habits, and masked.*

Moth. All hail, the richest beauties on the earth!

Boyet. Beauties no richer than rich taffeta.

Moth. A holy parcel of the fairest dames   160

              [*The ladies turn their backs to him.*

That ever turn'd their—backs—to mortal views!

Biron. [*Aside to Moth*] Their eyes, villain, their eyes.

Moth. That ever turn'd their eyes to mortal views!—
Out—

Boyet. True; out indeed.

Moth. Out of your favours, heavenly spirits, vouchsafe
Not to behold—

Biron. [*Aside to Moth*] Once to behold, rogue.

Moth. Once to behold with your sun-beamed eyes,
——with your sun-beamed eyes—   170

Boyet. They will not answer to that epithet;
You were best call it daughter-beamed eyes.

Moth. They do not mark me, and that brings me out.

Biron. Is this your perfectness? be gone, you rogue!

                 [*Exit Moth.*

Rosaline. What would these strangers? know their minds,
     Boyet.
If they do speak our language, 't is our will
That some plain man recount their purposes.
Know what they would.

Boyet. What would you with the princess?

Biron. Nothing but peace and gentle visitation.   180

Rosaline. What would they, say they?

Boyet. Nothing but peace and gentle visitation.

Rosaline. Why, that they have; and bid them so be gone.

Boyet. She says, you have it, and you may be gone.

King. Say to her, we have measur'd many miles
To tread a measure with her on this grass.

Boyet. They say, that they have measur'd many a mile
To tread a measure with you on this grass.

Rosaline. It is not so.   Ask them how many inches
Is in one mile ; if they have measur'd many,   190
The measure then of one is easily told.

Boyet. If to come hither you have measur'd miles,
And many miles, the princess bids you tell
How many inches doth fill up one mile.

Biron. Tell her, we measure them by weary steps.

Boyet. She hears herself.

Rosaline.   How many weary steps,
Of many weary miles you have o'ergone,
Are number'd in the travel of one mile?

Biron. We number nothing that we spend for you;
Our duty is so rich, so infinite,   200
That we may do it still without accompt.
Vouchsafe to show the sunshine of your face,
That we, like savages, may worship it.

Rosaline. My face is but a moon, and clouded too.

King. Blessed are clouds, to do as such clouds do!
Vouchsafe, bright moon,—and these thy stars,—to shine,
Those clouds remov'd, upon our watery eyne.

Rosaline. O vain petitioner! beg a greater matter;
Thou now request'st but moonshine in the water.

King. Then, in our measure vouchsafe but one change.
Thou bidst me beg; this begging is not strange.   211

Rosaline. Play, music, then!—Nay, you must do it soon.
                                        [*Music plays.*
Not yet,—no dance!—Thus change I like the moon.

King. Will you not dance? How come you thus estrang'd?

Rosaline. You took the moon at full, but now she 's chang'd.

King. Yet still she is the moon, and I the man.
The music plays; vouchsafe some motion to it.

Rosaline. Our ears vouchsafe it.

King.   But your legs should do it.

Rosaline. Since you are strangers and come here by
    chance,
We 'll not be nice; take hands.—We will not dance.   220
  King. Why take we hands, then?
  Rosaline.   Only to part friends.
Curtsy, sweet hearts; and so the measure ends.
  King. More measure of this measure; be not nice.
  Rosaline. We can afford no more at such a price.
  King. Prize you yourselves; what buys your company?
  Rosaline. Your absence only.
  King.   That can never be.
  Rosaline. Then cannot we be bought: and so, adieu;
Twice to your visor, and half once to you.
  King. If you deny to dance, let 's hold more chat.   229
  Rosaline. In private, then.
  King.   I am best pleas'd with that.
                    [They converse apart.

  Biron. White-handed mistress, one sweet word with thee.
  Princess. Honey, and milk, and sugar; there is three.
  Biron. Nay then, two treys, and if you grow so nice,
Metheglin, wort, and malmsey.   Well run, dice!
There 's half-a-dozen sweets.
  Princess.   Seventh sweet, adieu.
Since you can cog, I 'll play no more with you.
  Biron. One word in secret.
  Princess.   Let it not be sweet.
  Biron. Thou griev'st my gall.
  Princess.   Gall! bitter.
  Biron.   Therefore meet.
                    [They converse apart.
  Dumain. Will you vouchsafe with me to change a word?
  Maria. Name it.
  Dumain.   Fair lady,—
  Maria.   Say you so? Fair lord,—
Take that for your fair lady.

Dumain. Please it you, 241
As much in private, and I 'll bid adieu.

          [*They converse apart.*

Katherine. What, was your vizard made without a tongue?

Longaville. I know the reason, lady, why you ask.

Katherine. O, for your reason! quickly, sir; I long.

Longaville. You have a double tongue within your mask,
And would afford my speechless vizard half.

 Katherine. Veal, quoth the Dutchman.—Is not veal a calf?

 Longaville. A calf, fair lady!

 Katherine.   No, a fair lord calf.

 Longaville. Let 's part the word.

 Katherine.   No, I 'll not be your half.
Take all, and wean it; it may prove an ox. 251

 Longaville. Look, how you butt yourself in these sharp
  mocks!
Will you give horns, chaste lady? do not so.

 Katherine. Then die a calf, before your horns do grow.

 Longaville. One word in private with you, ere I die.

 Katherine. Bleat softly then; the butcher hears you cry.

          [*They converse apart.*

Boyet. The tongues of mocking wenches are as keen
 As is the razor's edge invisible,
Cutting a smaller hair than may be seen;
 Above the sense of sense, so sensible 260
Seemeth their conference; their conceits have wings
Fleeter than arrows, bullets, wind, thought, swifter things.

 Rosaline. Not one word more, my maids; break off, break
  off.

 Biron. By heaven, all dry-beaten with pure scoff!

 King. Farewell, mad wenches; you have simple wits.

 Princess. Twenty adieus, my frozen Muscovits.—

    [*Exeunt King, Lords, and Blackamoors.*
Are these the breed of wits so wonder'd at?

 Boyet. Tapers they are, with your sweet breaths puff'd out.

Rosaline. Well-liking wits they have ; gross, gross ; fat, fat.

   Princess. O poverty in wit, kingly-poor flout !   270

Will they not, think you, hang themselves to-night ?

Or ever, but in vizards, show their faces ?

This pert Biron was out of countenance quite.

   Rosaline. O, they were all in lamentable cases !

The king was weeping-ripe for a good word.

   Princess. Biron did swear himself out of all suit.

   Maria. Dumain was at my service, and his sword :

No point, quoth I ; my servant straight was mute.

   Katherine. Lord Longaville said I came o'er his heart ;

And trow you what he called me ?

   Princess.   Qualm, perhaps.   280

   Katherine. Yes, in good faith.

   Princess.   Go, sickness as thou art !

   Rosaline. Well, better wits have worn plain statute-caps.

But will you hear ? the king is my love sworn.

   Princess. And quick Biron hath plighted faith to me.

   Katherine. And Longaville was for my service born.

   Maria. Dumain is mine, as sure as bark on tree.

   Boyet. Madam, and pretty mistresses, give ear.

Immediately they will again be here

In their own shapes ; for it can never be

They will digest this harsh indignity.   290

   Princess. Will they return ?

   Boyet. They will, they will, God knows,

And leap for joy, though they are lame with blows.

Therefore change favours ; and, when they repair,

Blow like sweet roses in this summer air.

   Princess. How blow ? how blow ? speak to be understood.

   Boyet. Fair ladies mask'd are roses in their bud ;

Dismask'd, their damask sweet commixture shown,

Are angels vailing clouds, or roses blown.

   Princess. Avaunt, perplexity ! What shall we do,   300

If they return in their own shapes to woo ?

Rosaline. Good madam, if by me you 'll be advis'd,
Let 's mock them still, as well known as disguis'd.
Let us complain to them what fools were here,
Disguis'd like Muscovites, in shapeless gear;
And wonder what they were, and to what end
Their shallow shows, and prologue vilely penn'd,
And their rough carriage so ridiculous,
Should be presented at our tent to us.

   Boyet. Ladies, withdraw; the gallants are at hand.   310
   Princess. Whip to our tents, as roes run over land.

          [*Exeunt Princess, Rosaline, Katherine, and Maria.*

Re-enter the KING, BIRON, LONGAVILLE, *and* DUMAIN, *in their proper habits.*

   King. Fair sir, God save you! Where 's the princess?
   Boyet. Gone to her tent. Please it your majesty
Command me any service to her thither?
   King. That she vouchsafe me audience for one word.
   Boyet. I will; and so will she, I know, my lord.   [*Exit.*
   Biron. This fellow pecks up wit as pigeons pease,
And utters it again when God doth please.
He is wit's pedler, and retails his wares
At wakes and wassails, meetings, markets, fairs;   320
And we that sell by gross, the Lord doth know,
Have not the grace to grace it with such show.
This gallant pins the wenches on his sleeve;
Had he been Adam, he had tempted Eve.
He can carve too, and lisp: why, this is he
That kiss'd his hand away in courtesy;
This is the ape of form, monsieur the nice,
That, when he plays at tables, chides the dice
In honourable terms; nay, he can sing
A mean most meanly; and in ushering   330
Mend him who can: the ladies call him sweet;
The stairs, as he treads on them, kiss his feet.

This is the flower that smiles on every one,
To show his teeth as white as whale's bone;
And consciences, that will not die in debt,
Pay him the due of honey-tongu'd Boyet.
   King. A blister on his sweet tongue, with my heart,
That put Armado's page out of his part!
   Biron. See where it comes!—Behaviour, what wert thou
Till this man show'd thee? and what art thou now?   340

Re-enter the PRINCESS, *ushered by* BOYET; ROSALINE, MARIA,
and KATHERINE.

King. All hail, sweet madam, and fair time of day!
   Princess. Fair in all hail is foul, as I conceive.
King. Construe my speeches better, if you may.
   Princess. Then wish me better; I will give you leave.
King. We came to visit you, and purpose now
   To lead you to our court; vouchsafe it then.
Princess. This field shall hold me, and so hold your vow;
   Nor God, nor I, delights in perjur'd men.
King. Rebuke me not for that which you provoke;
   The virtue of your eye must break my oath.   350
Princess. You nickname virtue; vice you should have spoke,
   For virtue's office never breaks men's troth.
Now by my maiden honour, yet as pure
   As the unsullied lily, I protest,
A world of torments though I should endure,
   I would not yield to be your house's guest;
So much I hate a breaking cause to be
Of heavenly oaths, vow'd with integrity.
King. O, you have liv'd in desolation here,
   Unseen, unvisited, much to our shame.   360
Princess. Not so, my lord; it is not so, I swear;
   We have had pastimes here and pleasant game.
A mess of Russians left us but of late.
   King. How, madam! Russians!

Princess.   Ay, in truth, my lord;
Trim gallants, full of courtship and of state.
    Rosaline. Madam, speak true.—It is not so, my lord;
My lady, to the manner of the days,
In courtesy gives undeserving praise.
We four indeed confronted were with four
In Russian habit: here they stay'd an hour,   370
And talk'd apace; and in that hour, my lord,
They did not bless us with one happy word.
I dare not call them fools; but this I think,
When they are thirsty, fools would fain have drink.
    Biron. This jest is dry to me.—Fair gentle sweet,
Your wit makes wise things foolish: when we greet,
With eyes best seeing, heaven's fiery eye,
By light we lose light; your capacity
Is of that nature that to your huge store
Wise things seem foolish and rich things but poor.   380
    Rosaline. This proves you wise and rich, for in my eye,—
    Biron. I am a fool, and full of poverty.
    Rosaline. But that you take what doth to you belong,
It were a fault to snatch words from my tongue.
    Biron. O, I am yours, and all that I possess!
    Rosaline. All the fool mine?
    Biron.   I cannot give you less.
    Rosaline. Which of the vizards was it that you wore?
    Biron. Where? when? what vizard? why demand you this?
    Rosaline. There, then, that vizard; that superfluous case
That hid the worse and show'd the better face.   390
    King. [*Aside to Dumain*]. We are descried; they 'll mock
        us now downright.
    Dumain. [*Aside to King*] Let us confess and turn it to a jest.
    Princess. Amaz'd, my lord? why looks your highness sad?
    Rosaline. Help, hold his brows! he 'll swoon!—Why look
        you pale?—
Sea-sick, I think, coming from Muscovy.

Biron. Thus pour the stars down plagues for perjury.
  Can any face of brass hold longer out?—
Here stand I, lady: dart thy skill at me;
  Bruise me with scorn, confound me with a flout;
Thrust thy sharp wit quite through my ignorance; 40?
  Cut me to pieces with thy keen conceit;
And I will wish thee never more to dance,
  Nor never more in Russian habit wait.
O, never will I trust to speeches penn'd,
  Nor to the motion of a schoolboy's tongue,
Nor never come in vizard to my friend,
  Nor woo in rhyme, like a blind harper's song!
Taffeta phrases, silken terms precise,
  Three-pil'd hyperboles, spruce affectation,
Figures pedantical—these summer-flies 410
  Have blown me full of maggot ostentation.
I do forswear them; and I here protest,
  By this white glove,—how white the hand, God knows!—
Henceforth my wooing mind shall be express'd
  In russet yeas and honest kersey noes:
And to begin, wench,—so God help me, la!—
My love to thee is sound, sans crack or flaw.
  Rosaline. Sans sans, I pray you.
  Biron.   Yet I have a trick
Of the old rage: bear with me, I am sick;
I 'll leave it by degrees.   Soft, let us see: 420
Write, 'Lord have mercy on us' on those three;
They are infected; in their hearts it lies;
They have the plague, and caught it of your eyes;
These lords are visited; you are not free,
For the Lord's tokens on you do I see.
  Princess. No, they are free that gave these tokens to us.
  Biron. Our states are forfeit; seek not to undo us.
  Rosaline. It is not so; for how can this be true,
That you stand forfeit, being those that sue.

Biron. Peace! for I will not have to do with you.   430
Rosaline. Nor shall not, if I do as I intend.
Biron. Speak for yourselves; my wit is at an end.
King. Teach us, sweet madam, for our rude transgression
Some fair excuse.
Princess.   The fairest is confession.
Were not you here but even now disguis'd?
King. Madam, I was.
Princess.   And were you well advis'd?
King. I was, fair madam.
Princess.   When you then were here,
What did you whisper in your lady's ear?
King. That more than all the world I did respect her.
Princess. When she shall challenge this, you will reject her.
King. Upon mine honour, no.
Princess.   Peace, peace! forbear;
Your oath once broke, you force not to forswear.   442
King. Despise me, when I break this oath of mine.
Princess. I will; and therefore keep it.—Rosaline,
What did the Russian whisper in your ear?
Rosaline. Madam, he swore that he did hold me dear
As precious eyesight, and did value me
Above this world; adding thereto moreover
That he would wed me, or else die my lover.
Princess. God give thee joy of him! the noble lord   450
Most honourably doth uphold his word.
King. What mean you, madam? by my life, my troth,
I never swore this lady such an oath.
Rosaline. By heaven, you did; and to confirm it plain,
You gave me this: but take it, sir, again.
King. My faith and this the princess I did give;
I knew her by this jewel on her sleeve.
Princess. Pardon me, sir, this jewel did she wear;
And Lord Biron, I thank him, is my dear.—
What, will you have me, or your pearl again?   460

Biron. Neither of either; I remit both twain.—
I see the trick on 't; here was a consent,
Knowing aforehand of our merriment,
To dash it like a Christmas comedy.
Some carry-tale, some please-man, some slight zany,
Some mumble-news, some trencher-knight, some Dick,
That smiles his cheek in years and knows the trick
To make my lady laugh when she 's dispos'd,
Told our intents before; which once disclos'd,
The ladies did change favours, and then we,   470
Following the signs, woo'd but the sign of she.
Now, to our perjury to add more terror,
We are again forsworn,—in will, and error.
Much upon this it is.—And might not you   [*To Boyet.*
Forestall our sport, to make us thus untrue?
Do not you know my lady's foot by the squire,
    And laugh upon the apple of her eye?
And stand between her back, sir, and the fire,
    Holding a trencher, jesting merrily?
You put our page out: go, you are allow'd;   480
Die when you will, a smock shall be your shroud.
You leer upon me, do you? there 's an eye
Wounds like a leaden sword.
    Boyet.   Full merrily
Hath this brave manage, this career, been run.
    Biron. Lo, he is tilting straight! Peace! I have done.—

Enter COSTARD.

Welcome, pure wit! thou partest a fair fray.
    Costard. O Lord, sir, they would know
Whether the three Worthies shall come in or no.
    Biron. What, are there but three?
    Costard.   No, sir; but it is vara fine,
For every one pursents three.
    Biron.   And three times thrice is nine.

Costard. Not so, sir; under correction, sir; I hope it is
    not so.   491
You cannot beg us, sir, I can assure you, sir; we know what
    we know:
I hope, sir, three times thrice, sir,—

Biron. Is not nine.

Costard. Under correction, sir, we know whereuntil it doth
amount.

Biron. By Jove, I always took three threes for nine.

Costard. O Lord, sir, it were pity you should get your living by reckoning, sir.

Biron. How much is it?   500

Costard. O Lord, sir, the parties themselves, the actors,
sir, will show whereuntil it doth amount; for mine own part,
I am, as they say, but to pursent one man,—e'en one poor
man—Pompion the Great, sir.

Biron. Art thou one of the Worthies?

Costard. It pleased them to think me worthy of Pompion
the Great; for mine own part, I know not the degree of the
Worthy, but I am to stand for him.

Biron. Go, bid them prepare.   509

Costard. We will turn it finely off, sir; we will take some
    care.   [*Exit.*

King. Biron, they will shame us; let them not approach.

Biron. We are shame-proof, my lord; and 't is some policy
To have one show worse than the king's and his company.

King. I say they shall not come.

Princess. Nay, my good lord, let me o'errule you now;
That sport best pleases that doth least know how.
Where zeal strives to content, and the contents
Dies in the zeal of that which it presents,
Their form confounded makes most form in mirth,
When great things labouring perish in their birth.   520

Biron. A right description of our sport, my lord.

Enter ARMADO.

Armado. Anointed, I implore so much expense of thy royal
sweet breath as will utter a brace of words.

　　[*Converses apart with the King, and delivers him a paper.*
Princess. Doth this man serve God?

Biron. Why ask you.

Princess. He speaks not like a man of God's making.

Armado. That is all one, my fair, sweet, honey monarch;
for, I protest, the schoolmaster is exceeding fantastical, too
too vain, too too vain: but we will put it, as they say, to fortuna de la guerra.   I wish you the peace of mind, most royal
couplement!   [*Exit.*

King. Here is like to be a good presence of Worthies.
He presents Hector of Troy; the swain, Pompey the Great;
the parish curate, Alexander; Armado's page, Hercules; the
pedant, Judas Maccabæus:
And if these four Worthies in their first show thrive,
These four will change habits, and present the other five.

Biron. There is five in the first show.

King. You are deceived; 't is not so.

Biron. The pedant, the braggart, the hedge-priest, the fool,
and the boy.—   541
Abate throw at novum, and the whole world again
Cannot pick out five such, take each one in his vein.

King. The ship is under sail, and here she comes amain.

Enter COSTARD, *for Pompey.*

Costard. I Pompey am,—

Boyet.　　　　　　　You lie, you are not he.

Costard. I Pompey am,—

Boyet.　　　　　　　With libbard's head on knee.

Biron. Well said, old mocker; I must needs be friends
　　with thee.

Costard. I Pompey am, Pompey surnam'd the Big,—

Dumain. The Great.

Costard. It is Great, sir:—

Pompey surnam'd the Great;   550
That oft in field, with targe and shield, did make my foe to sweat:
And travelling along this coast, I here am come by chance,
And lay my arms before the legs of this sweet lass of France.—

If your ladyship would say, 'Thanks, Pompey,' I had done.

Princess. Great thanks, great Pompey.

Costard. 'T is not so much worth; but I hope I was perfect. I made a little fault in 'Great.'

Biron. My hat to a halfpenny, Pompey proves the best
Worthy.

Enter SIR NATHANIEL, *for Alexander.*

Nathaniel. When in the world I liv'd, I was the world's com-
        mander;   560
By east, west, north, and south, I spread my conquering might;
My scutcheon plain declares that I am Alisander,—

Boyet. Your nose says, no, you are not; for it stands too
        right.

Biron. Your nose smells no in this, most tender-smelling
        knight.

Princess. The conqueror is dismay'd.—Proceed, good Alex-
        ander.

Nathaniel. When in the world I liv'd, I was the world's com-
        mander,—

Boyet. Most true, 't is right; you were so, Alisander.

Biron. Pompey the Great,—

Costard. Your servant, and Costard.   569

Biron. Take away the conqueror, take away Alisander.

Costard. [*To Sir Nathaniel*] O, sir, you have overthrown
Alisander the conqueror! You will be scraped out of the
painted cloth for this: your lion, that holds his poll-axe sitting on a close-stool, will be given to Ajax; he will be the
ninth Worthy. A conqueror, and afeard to speak! run away
for shame, Alisander.—[*Nathaniel retires.*] There, an 't shall
please you; a foolish mild man; an honest man, look you,

and soon dashed. He is a marvellous good neighbour, faith, and a very good bowler; but, for Alisander,—alas, you see how 't is,—a little o'erparted.—But there are Worthies a-coming will speak their mind in some other sort. 581

Princess. Stand aside, good Pompey.

Enter HOLOFERNES, *for Judas; and* MOTH, *for Hercules.*

Holofernes. Great Hercules is presented by this imp,
    Whose club kill'd Cerberus, that three-headed canus;
And when he was a babe, a child, a shrimp,
    Thus did he strangle serpents in his manus.
Quoniam he seemeth in minority,
Ergo I come with this apology.—
Keep some state in thy exit, and vanish.—   [*Moth retires.*
    Judas I am,—   590
Dumain. A Judas!
Holofernes. Not Iscariot, sir.—
    Judas I am, ycliped Maccabæus.
Dumain. Judas Maccabæus clipt is plain Judas.
Biron. A kissing traitor.—How art thou prov'd Judas?
Holofernes. Judas I am,—
Dumain. The more shame for you, Judas.
Holofernes. What mean you, sir?
Boyet. To make Judas hang himself.
Holofernes. Begin, sir; you are my elder.   600
Biron. Well follow'd; Judas was hang'd on an elder.
Holofernes. I will not be put out of countenance.
Biron. Because thou hast no face.
Holofernes. What is this?
Boyet. A cittern-head.
Dumain. The head of a bodkin.
Biron. A Death's face in a ring.
Longaville. The face of an old Roman coin, scarce seen.
Boyet. The pommel of Cæsar's falchion.
Dumain. The carved-bone face on a flask.   610
Biron. Saint George's half-check in a brooch.

H

Dumain. Ay, and in a brooch of lead.

Biron. Ay, and worn in the cap of a tooth-drawer.—
And now forward; for we have put thee in countenance.

Holofernes. You have put me out of countenance.

Biron. False; we have given thee faces.

Holofernes. But you have out-faced them all.

Biron. An thou wert a lion, we would do so.

Boyet. Therefore, as he is an ass, let him go.—
And so adieu, sweet Jude! nay, why dost thou stay?   620

Dumain. For the latter end of his name.

Biron. For the ass to the Jude? give it him.—Jud-as,
away!

Holofernes. This is not generous, not gentle, not humble.

Boyet. A light for Monsieur Judas! it grows dark, he may
stumble.   [*Holofernes retires.*

Princess. Alas, poor Maccabæus, how hath he been baited!

Enter ARMADO, *for Hector.*

Biron. Hide thy head, Achilles; here comes Hector in
arms.

Dumain. Though my mocks come home by me, I will
now be merry.

King. Hector was but a Trojan in respect of this.   630

Boyet. But is this Hector?

King. I think Hector was not so clean-timbered.

Longaville. His leg is too big for Hector's.

Dumain. More calf, certain.

Boyet. No; he is best indued in the small.

Biron. This cannot be Hector.

Dumain. He's a god or a painter; for he makes faces.

Armado. The armipotent Mars, of lances the almighty,
Gave Hector a gift,—

Dumain. A gilt nutmeg.   640

Biron. A lemon.

Longaville. Stuck with cloves.

Dumain. No, cloven.

Armado. Peace !—

The armipotent Mars, of lances the almighty,
    Gave Hector a gift, the heir of Ilion ;
A man so breath'd, that certain he would fight ye
    From morn till night, out of his pavilion.

I am that flower,—

Dumain.   That mint.

Longaville.   That columbine.

Armado. Sweet Lord Longaville, rein thy tongue.   650

Longaville. I must rather give it the rein, for it runs against Hector.

Dumain. Ay, and Hector 's a greyhound.

Armado. The sweet war-man is dead and rotten ; sweet chucks, beat not the bones of the buried : when he breathed, he was a man. But I will forward with my device.—[*To the Princess*] Sweet royalty, bestow on me the sense of hearing.

Princess. Speak, brave Hector ; we are much delighted.

Armado. I do adore thy sweet grace's slipper.

Boyet. [*Aside to Dumain*] Loves her by the foot.   660

Dumain. [*Aside to Boyet*] He may not by the yard.

Armado. This Hector far surmounted Hannibal,—

Costard. The party is gone, fellow Hector, she is gone ; she is two months on her way.

Armado. What meanest thou ?

Costard. Faith, unless you play the honest Trojan, the poor wench is cast away ; she 's quick.

Armado. Dost thou infamonize me among potentates ? thou shalt die.   669

Costard. Then shall Hector be whipped for Jaquenetta that is quick by him, and hanged for Pompey that is dead by him.

Dumain. Most rare Pompey !

Boyet. Renowned Pompey !

Biron. Greater than great,--great, great, great Pompey ! Pompey the Huge !

Dumain. Hector trembles.

Biron. Pompey is moved.—More Ates, more Ates! stir
them on! stir them on!

Dumain. Hector will challenge him.   680

Biron. Ay, if he have no more man's blood in 's belly than
will sup a flea.

Armado. By the north pole, I do challenge thee.

Costard. I will not fight with a pole, like a northern man:
I 'll slash; I 'll do it by the sword. I pray you, let me bor-
row my arms again.

Dumain. Room for the incensed Worthies.

Costard. I 'll do it in my shirt.

Dumain. Most resolute Pompey!   689

Moth. Master, let me take you a button-hole lower. Do
you not see Pompey is uncasing for the combat? What
mean you? You will lose your reputation.

Armado. Gentlemen and soldiers, pardon me; I will not
combat in my shirt.

Dumain. You may not deny it; Pompey hath made the
challenge.

Armado. Sweet bloods, I both may and will.

Biron. What reason have you for 't?

Armado. The naked truth of it is, I have no shirt; I go
woolward for penance.   700

Boyet. True, and it was enjoined him in Rome for want
of linen; since when, I 'll be sworn, he wore none but a
dishclout of Jaquenetta's, and that he wears next his heart
for a favour.

Enter MERCADE.

Mercade. God save you, madam!

Princess. Welcome, Mercade,
But that thou interrupt'st our merriment.

Mercade. I am sorry, madam, for the news I bring
Is heavy in my tongue. The king your father—

Princess. Dead, for my life!   710

Mercade. Even so; my tale is told.

Biron. Worthies, away! the scene begins to cloud.

Armado. For mine own part, I breathe free breath. I have seen the day of wrong through the little hole of discretion, and I will right myself like a soldier.

[*Exeunt Worthies.*

King. How fares your majesty?

Princess. Boyet, prepare; I will away to-night.

King. Madam, not so; I do beseech you, stay.

Princess. Prepare, I say.—I thank you, gracious lords,
For all your fair endeavours, and entreat,   720
Out of a new-sad soul, that you vouchsafe
In your rich wisdom to excuse or hide
The liberal opposition of our spirits;
If over-boldly we have borne ourselves
In the converse of breath, your gentleness
Was guilty of it.—Farewell, worthy lord!
A heavy heart bears not a nimble tongue.
Excuse me so, coming too short of thanks
For my great suit so easily obtain'd.

King. The extreme parts of time extremely forms   730
All causes to the purpose of his speed,
And often at his very loose decides
That which long process could not arbitrate:
And though the mourning brow of progeny
Forbid the smiling courtesy of love
The holy suit which fain it would convince,
Yet, since love's argument was first on foot,
Let not the cloud of sorrow justle it
From what it purpos'd; since, to wail friends lost
Is not by much so wholesome-profitable   740
As to rejoice at friends but newly found.

Princess. I understand you not; my griefs are dull.

Biron. Honest plain words best pierce the ear of grief;
And by these badges understand the king.

For your fair sakes have we neglected time,
Play'd foul play with our oaths: your beauty, ladies,
Hath much deform'd us, fashioning our humours
Even to the opposed end of our intents;
And what in us hath seem'd ridiculous,—
As love is full of unbefitting strains,   750
All wanton as a child, skipping and vain,
Form'd by the eye, and therefore, like the eye,
Full of strange shapes, of habits, and of forms,
Varying in subjects as the eye doth roll
To every varied object in his glance:
Which parti-coated presence of loose love
Put on by us, if, in your heavenly eyes,
Have misbecom'd our oaths and gravities,
Those heavenly eyes, that look into these faults,
Suggested us to make.   Therefore, ladies,   760
Our love being yours, the error that love makes
Is likewise yours: we to ourselves prove false,
By being once false for ever to be true
To those that make us both,—fair ladies, you;
And even that falsehood, in itself a sin,
Thus purifies itself and turns to grace.
    Princess. We have receiv'd your letters full of love,
Your favours, the ambassadors of love,
And, in our maiden council, rated them
At courtship, pleasant jest, and courtesy,   770
As bombast and as lining to the time;
But more devout than this in our respects
Have we not been, and therefore met your loves
In their own fashion, like a merriment.
    Dumain. Our letters, madam, show'd much more than jest.
    Longaville. So did our looks.
    Rosaline.   We did not quote them so.
    King. Now, at the latest minute of the hour,
Grant us your loves.

Princess.   A time, methinks, too short
To make a world-without-end bargain in.
No, no, my lord, your grace is perjur'd much,   780
Full of dear guiltiness; and therefore this:
If for my love—as there is no such cause—
You will do aught, this shall you do for me:
Your oath I will not trust; but go with speed
To some forlorn and naked hermitage,
Remote from all the pleasures of the world;
There stay until the twelve celestial signs
Have brought about the annual reckoning.
If this austere insociable life
Change not your offer made in heat of blood,   790
If frosts and fasts, hard lodging and thin weeds
Nip not the gaudy blossoms of your love,
But that it bear this trial and last love,
Then, at the expiration of the year,
Come challenge me, challenge me by these deserts,
And, by this virgin palm now kissing thine,
I will be thine, and till that instant shut
My woeful self up in a mourning house,
Raining the tears of lamentation
For the remembrance of my father's death.   800
If this thou do deny, let our hands part,
Neither intitled in the other's heart.
King. If this, or more than this, I would deny,
   To flatter up these powers of mine with rest,
The sudden hand of death close up mine eye!
   Hence ever then my heart is in thy breast.
   [*Biron.* And what to me, my love? and what to me?
   Rosaline. You must be purged too, your sins are rank,
You are attaint with faults and perjury;
Therefore if you my favour mean to get,   810
A twelvemonth shall you spend, and never rest,
But seek the weary beds of people sick.]

Dumain. But what to me, my love? but what to me?
A wife?

Katherine. A beard, fair health, and honesty;
With three-fold love I wish you all these three.

Dumain. O, shall I say, I thank you, gentle wife?

Katherine. Not so, my lord; a twelvemonth and a day
I 'll mark no words that smooth-fac'd wooers say.
Come when the king doth to my lady come;
Then, if I have much love, I 'll give you some.   820

Dumain. I 'll serve thee true and faithfully till then.

Katherine. Yet swear not, lest ye be forsworn again.

Longaville. What says Maria?

Maria.   At the twelvemonth's end
I 'll change my black gown for a faithful friend.

Longaville. I 'll stay with patience; but the time is
    long.

Maria. The liker you; few taller are so young.

Biron. Studies my lady? mistress, look on me;
Behold the window of my heart, mine eye,
What humble suit attends thy answer there;
Impose some service on me for thy love.   830

Rosaline. Oft have I heard of you, my Lord Biron,
Before I saw you; and the world's large tongue
Proclaims you for a man replete with mocks,
Full of comparisons and wounding flouts,
Which you on all estates will execute
That lie within the mercy of your wit.
To weed this wormwood from your fruitful brain,
And therewithal to win me, if you please,—
Without the which I am not to be won,—
You shall this twelvemonth term from day to day   840
Visit the speechless sick, and still converse
With groaning wretches; and your task shall be,
With all the fierce endeavour of your wit
To enforce the pained impotent to smile.

Biron. To move wild laughter in the throat of death?
It cannot be; it is impossible:
Mirth cannot move a soul in agony.

   Rosaline. Why, that 's the way to choke a gibing spirit,
Whose influence is begot of that loose grace
Which shallow laughing hearers give to fools.   850
A jest's prosperity lies in the ear
Of him that hears it, never in the tongue
Of him that makes it: then, if sickly ears,
Deaf'd with the clamours of their own dear groans,
Will hear your idle scorns, continue them,
And I will have you and that fault withal;
But if they will not, throw away that spirit,
And I shall find you empty of that fault,
Right joyful of your reformation.

   Biron. A twelvemonth! well; befall what will befall,   860
I 'll jest a twelvemonth in an hospital.

   Princess. [*To the King*] Ay, sweet my lord; and so I take
     my leave.

   King. No, madam; we will bring you on your way.

   Biron. Our wooing doth not end like an old play;
Jack hath not Jill: these ladies' courtesy
Might well have made our sport a comedy.

   King. Come, sir, it wants a twelvemonth and a day,
And then 't will end.

   Biron.   That 's too long for a play.

            Re-enter ARMADO.

   Armado. Sweet majesty, vouchsafe me,—

   Princess. Was not that Hector?   870

   Dumain. The worthy knight of Troy.

   Armado. I will kiss thy royal finger, and take leave. I
am a votary; I have vowed to Jaquenetta to hold the plough
for her sweet love three years. But, most esteemed greatness, will you hear the dialogue that the two learned men

have compiled in praise of the owl and the cuckoo? it should
have followed in the end of our show.

King. Call them forth quickly; we will do so.

Armado. Holla! approach.

Re-enter HOLOFERNES, NATHANIEL, MOTH, COSTARD, *and others.*

This side is Hiems, Winter, this Ver, the Spring; the one
maintained by the owl, the other by the cuckoo.—Ver, begin.

Song.

Spring. *When daisies pied and violets blue,*   882
   And lady-smocks all silver-white,
 And cuckoo-buds of yellow hue
   Do paint the meadows with delight,
 The cuckoo, then, on every tree,
 Mocks married men; for thus sings he,
    Cuckoo;
 Cuckoo, cuckoo,—O word of fear,
 Unpleasing to a married ear!   890

 When shepherds pipe on oaten straws,
  And merry larks are ploughmen's clocks,
 When turtles tread, and rooks, and daws,
  And maidens bleach their summer smocks,
 The cuckoo then, on every tree,
 Mocks married men; for thus sings he,
    Cuckoo;
 Cuckoo, cuckoo,—O word of fear,
 Unpleasing to a married ear!

Winter. *When icicles hang by the wall,*   900
   And Dick the shepherd blows his nail,
 And Tom bears logs into the hall,
   And milk comes frozen home in pail,
 When blood is nipp'd and ways be foul,

Then nightly sings the staring owl,
        Tu-whoo;
Tu-whit, tu-whoo, a merry note,
While greasy Joan doth keel the pot.

When all aloud the wind doth blow,
    And coughing drowns the parson's saw,   910
And birds sit brooding in the snow,
    And Marian's nose looks red and raw,
When roasted crabs hiss in the bowl,
Then nightly sings the staring owl,
        Tu-whoo;
Tu-whit, tu-whoo, a merry note,
While greasy Joan doth keel the pot.

Armado. The words of Mercury are harsh after the songs of Apollo.   You that way,—we this way.   [*Exeunt.*

CHÂTEAU OF HENRY IV., PAU (THE OLD CAPITAL OF NAVARRE).

NOTES.

ABBREVIATIONS USED IN THE NOTES.

Abbott (or Gr.), Abbott's *Shakespearian Grammar* (third edition).

A. S., Anglo-Saxon.

A. V., Authorized Version of the Bible (1611).

B. and F., Beaumont and Fletcher.

B. J., Ben Jonson.

Camb. ed., "Cambridge edition" of Shakespeare, edited by Clark and Wright.

Cf. (*confer*), compare.

Clarke, "Cassell's Illustrated Shakespeare," edited by Charles and Mary Cowden-Clarke (London, n. d.).

Coll., Collier (second edition).

Coll. MS., Manuscript Corrections of Second Folio, edited by Collier.

D., Dyce (second edition).

H., Hudson ("Harvard" edition).

Halliwell, J. O. Halliwell (folio ed. of Shakespeare).

Id. (*idem*), the same.

K., Knight (second edition).

Nares, *Glossary*, edited by Halliwell and Wright (London, 1859).

Prol., Prologue.

S., Shakespeare.

Schmidt, A. Schmidt's *Shakespeare-Lexicon* (Berlin, 1874).

Sr., Singer.

St., Staunton.

Theo., Theobald.

V., Verplanck.

W., R. Grant White.

Walker, Wm. Sidney Walker's *Critical Examination of the Text of Shakespeare* (London, 1860).

Warb., Warburton.

Wb., Webster's Dictionary (revised quarto edition of 1879).

Worc., Worcester's Dictionary (quarto edition).

The abbreviations of the names of Shakespeare's Plays will be readily understood; as *T. N.* for *Twelfth Night, Cor.* for *Coriolanus*, 3 *Hen. VI.* for *The Third Part of King Henry the Sixth*, etc. *P. P.* refers to *The Passionate Pilgrim; V. and A.* to *Venus and Adonis; L. C.* to *Lover's Complaint;* and *Sonn.* to the *Sonnets.*

When the abbreviation of the name of a play is followed by a reference to *page,* Rolfe's edition of the play is meant.

The numbers of the lines (except for the present play) are those of the "Globe" ed.

NOTES.

Like Muscovites or Russians (v. 2. 121).

INTRODUCTION.

THE TITLE OF THE PLAY.—Mason says: "I believe the title of this play should be *Love's Labours Lost*," and Mr. Furnivall (see p. 9 above) agrees with him. The title-pages of the quartos give "Loues labors lost" and "Loues Labours lost;" but the running title of the quartos and 1st and 2d folios is "Loues Labour 's Lost," which is clearly a contraction of "Love's Labour is Lost." In the early eds. the possessive case is commonly given without the apostrophe (as in the titles "A Midsommer nights Dreame" and "The Winters Tale"); but the contraction of *is* generally has the apostrophe (as in "All's Well that ends Well"). Meres calls the play "Loue labors lost," and Tofte "Loues Labour Lost." We prefer to follow the folio rather than the quarto, which is not consistent with itself.

In the quartos the play is not divided into acts or scenes. In the folio it is divided into acts of very unequal length, "the first being half as long again, the fourth twice as long, the fifth three times as long, as the second and third" (Spedding).

DRAMATIS PERSONÆ.—In the quartos and the folio (cf. *Oth.* p. 153) no list of *dramatis personæ* is given. *Biron* is spelt "Berowne," and in iv. 3. 227 it rhymes with "moon." W. spells it "Birone." *Mercade* appears as "Marcade" in the quartos and 1st folio, and *Armado* is sometimes "Armatho." W. thinks that *Moth* should be printed "Mote," as it was clearly so pronounced. Cf. *A. Y. L.* p. 179 (note on *Goats*) and *Much Ado*, p. 136 (on *Nothing*). In i. 2. 85 of the present play, in "She had a green wit" there is probably an allusion to the "green withes" used in binding Samson. *Boyet* rhymes with *debt* in v. 2. 336; *Longaville* with *ill* in iv. 3. 118, and with *mile* in v. 2. 53; and *Rosaline* with *thine* in iv. 3. 216. Costard, in the old stage-directions, is called "Clown."

COSTUME.—As K. remarks, Cesare Vecellio, in his *Habiti Antichi* (ed. 1598), gives us the general costume of Navarre at this period. We are told that some dressed in imitation of the French, and some in the style of the Spaniards, while others blended the fashions of both these nations. The cut on p. 9 is from Vecellio, and shows the Spanish gentleman and the French lady of 1589. For the costume of the Muscovites in the masque, see on v. 2. 121 below, and cf. cut on p. 127.

ACT I.

SCENE I.—3. *And then*, etc. Pope puts this line in the margin as spurious.

6. *Bate.* Blunt; not to be printed "'bate," as by H. and some other editors. Cf. *bateless* in *R. of L.* 9: "bateless edge;" and *unbated* in *Ham.* iv. 7. 139: "A sword unbated;" and *Id.* v. 2. 328: "Unbated and envenom'd."

11. *Edict.* Accented by S. on either syllable, as suits the measure. Cf. the present instance and *M. N. D.* i. 1. 151 with *Rich. III.* i. 4. 203, etc.

13. *Academe.* The spelling of the 2d quarto and 2d folio; the 1st quarto and 1st folio have "Achademe," and the 3d and 4th folios "Academy."

14. *Living art.* "Immortal science" (Schmidt). For *art* = letters, learning in general, cf. iv. 2. 106 below.

23. *Deep oaths.* For the use of *deep*, cf. *Sonn.* 152. 9: "I have sworn deep oaths;" *R. of L.* 1847: "that deep vow;" and *K. John*, iii. 1. 231: "deep-sworn faith."

Steevens changed *oaths* to "oath" on account of the following *it ;* but, as the Camb. editors remark, we have here "an instance of the lax grammar of the time, which permitted the use of a singular pronoun referring to a plural substantive, and vice versa." Cf. *Two Noble Kinsmen,* i. 1 :

> "You cannot read *it* there ; there, through my tears,
>   Like wrinkled pebbles in a glassy stream,
>   You may behold *'em."*

The second folio changes *it* to "them." We may explain *it* as ="that which you have vowed to do" (Clarke).

27. *Bankrupt quite.* The 1st quarto has "bancrout quite," the folios only "bankerout." Pope was the first modern editor to restore *quite.* For the spelling of *bankrupt,* see *R. and J.* p. 187.

29. *These world's delights.* These worldly delights. The Coll. MS. changes *these* to "this."

32. *All these.* That is, his companions, to whom he may be supposed to point. Johnson took *these* to refer to *love, wealth,* and *pomp.* Mr. P. A. Daniel conjectures "all three."

43. *Wink.* Shut the eyes ; as often in S. Cf. *Sonn.* 43. 1, 56. 6, *Temp.* ii. 1. 216, *C. of E.* iii. 2. 58, etc.

For *of*=during, cf. *T. of S.* ind. 2. 84 : "But did I never speak of all that time ?" Gr. 176.

50. *An if.* For *an if* or *and if* (=even if), see Gr. 105.

62. *Feast.* The quartos and folios all have "fast ;" corrected by Theo. He suggested as an alternative "fore-bid" (="enjoined beforehand") for *forbid.*

64. *From common sense.* That is, from ordinary sight or perception. Cf. "the sense of sense" (=the sight of the eye) in v. 2. 260 below.

65. *Too hard a keeping oath.* For the transposition of the article, cf. *K. John,* iv. 2. 27 : "So new a fashion'd robe ;" *C. of E.* iii. 2. 186 : "so fair an offer'd chain ;" *T. and C.* v. 6. 20 : "much more a fresher man," etc. Gr. 422. Most editors follow Hanmer in printing "hard-a-keeping."

67. *Be thus.* Changed by Pope to "be this."

72. *And that.* The reading of the folios ; the 1st quarto has "but that."

80. *Study me.* The *me* is the expletive pronoun, or "dativus ethicus," often used, as here, "with a slight dash of humour" (H.). Cf. Gr. 220.

82. *Who dazzling so,* etc. "That when he *dazzles,* that is, has his eye made weak, by fixing his eye upon a fairer eye, that *fairer* eye shall be his *heed,* his *direction* or *lodestar,* and give him light that was blinded by it" (Johnson).

87. *Base.* Perhaps, as Walker conjectures, a misprint for "bare."

91. *Wot.* Know ; used only in the present and the participle *wotting,* for which see *W. T.* p. 175.

92. *Too much to know,* etc. "The consequence, says Biron, of too much knowledge, is not any real solution of doubts, but mere reputation ; that is, too much knowledge gives only *fame,* a name which every godfather can give likewise" (Johnson) ; or, as Clarke puts it : "To know overmuch is not to be wise, but to get the name of being wise : and ev-

ery godfather (like *these earthly godfathers* that name the stars) can give a man a name for wisdom."

95. *Proceeded well*, etc. There is a play upon *proceed*, which, as Johnson notes, is "an academical term, meaning to take a degree, as *he proceeded bachelor in physic*."

100. *Sneaping*. Snipping, or nipping. Cf. *W. T.* i. 2. 13: "Sneaping winds;" and *R. of L.* 333: "the sneaped birds." For the noun *sneap* (=snubbing) see 2 *Hen. IV.* p. 161.

104. *An abortive*. The early eds. have "any" for *an;* corrected by Pope. The error was probably due to the *any* in the line above.

106. *Mirth*. The early eds. have "showes" or "shows." Theo. substituted "earth" for the sake of the rhyme, but we prefer Walker's conjecture of *mirth*. Malone thinks that a line rhyming with 104 may have been lost.

107. *Like of*. Cf. *Much Ado*, v. 4. 59: "I am your husband, if you like of me." See also iv. 3. 153 below. Gr. 177.

108. *So you, to study*, etc. This is the quarto reading, and is generally adopted, though we cannot help thinking that there is some corruption. The folio has:

> "So you to studie now it is too late,
> That were to clymbe ore the house to vnlocke the gate."

W. reads:

> "So you to study now;—it is too late:
> That were to climb the house o'er to unlock the gate;"

which he explains thus: "Birone, in justification of his ridicule of these literary pursuits, says that they are untimely, that he likes not roses at Christmas or snow in May, and adds, 'So it is too late for you to study now: that were to climb over a house to unlock a gate; or, in other words, 'you are beginning at the wrong end—doing boys' work at men's years.' But, according to the quarto, he says, 'I like of each thing that in season grows; *so* you, now it is too late to study, climb o'er the house to unlock the little gate:' whereas it was not *so* (that is, like Birone) at all, but exactly *not* so." We take it, however, that *to study now it is too late* is = in studying now that it is too late; the infinitive being used in the "indefinite" way, as Abbott calls it (Gr. 356), so common in S. But, as Lettsom has noted, the *so* is awkward in either case. He conjectures:

> "But you 'll to study, now it is too late;
> That were to climb o'er the house to unlock the gate."

If the folio is to be followed, it is better to take it just as it is, making it a line of five feet with slurred syllables, than to turn it into an alexandrine, as W. does. Alexandrines are extremely rare in the early plays of S. Mr. Fleay (Dr. Ingleby's *S. the Man and the Book*, Part II. p. 71) finds only four in *L. L. L.*, one of which is doubtful. The Coll. MS. has "by study" for *to study*, and "Climb o'er the house-top to unlock the gate."

110. *Sit you out*. The reading of the quartos and the later folios; the 1st folio has "fit" for *sit*. The expression is one used in card-playing for taking no part in the game.

114. *Swore*. The reading of the later folios, and required by the rhyme.

The quartos and 1st folio have "sworne." Elsewhere S. has *sworn* for the participle, but we find *broke* for *broken, froze* for *frozen, smote* for *smitten,* etc. See Gr. 343. Cf. *forgot* in 139 below, and *chose* in 167.

127. *Gentility.* Refinement, courtesy. Theo. conjectures "garrulity," and St. "scurrility." II. points thus : " A dangerous law,—against gentility." The early eds. make the line a part of Longaville's speech ; but Theo. is clearly right in transferring it to Biron.

134. *Complete.* Accented on the first syllable because preceding a noun so accented. See *M. for M.* p. 139, and cf. *Cymb.* p. 174 (on *Supreme*) or *Cor.* p. 255 (on *Divine*).

145. *Of force.* Perforce, of necessity.

146. *Lie.* Lodge, reside. See 2 *Hen. IV.* p. 185, or *Oth.* p. 193. Reed quotes Wotton's definition : " An ambassador is an honest man sent to lie abroad for the good of his country."

Mere. Absolute. See *Temp.* p. 111, note on *We are merely cheated,* etc. Cf. i. 2. 33 below.

149. *Affects.* Affections, inclinations ; as in *Rich. II.* 1. 4. 30 and *Oth.* i. 3. 264.

156. *Suggestions.* Temptations ; the usual meaning in S. See *Temp.* p. 127. Cf. the verb in v. 2. 760 below.

158. *I am the last that will last keep his oath.* Mr. P. A. Daniel conjectures " one " for the first *last,* on the ground that Biron is made to say the contrary of what he means; but S. sometimes twists the sense of a word a little for the sake of a repetition like this. Walker would read " last will " for *will last.*

159. *Quick.* Lively, animated ; as in i. 2. 23, 29, v. 1. 54, and v. 2. 284 below. Cf. its use =living ; for which see *Ham.* p. 262.

164. *One whom.* The 1st folio has "One who," which might be retained. Cf. iv. 1. 71 below, and see Gr. 274.

166. *Complements.* Probably =accomplishments, as Johnson and others explain it. Schmidt takes it to be =external show. The early eds. make no distinction between *complement* and *compliment.*

168. *Hight.* Is called ; used by S. only as an archaism. Cf. 245 below. See also *M. N. D.* v. 1. 140 and *Per.* iv. prol. 18.

171. *Debate.* Contest, quarrel ; the only sense in S. Cf. *M. N. D.* ii. 1. 116, 2 *Hen. IV.* iv. 4. 2, etc.

174. *I will use him for my minstrelsy.* " I will make a *minstrel* of him, whose occupation was to relate fabulous stories " (Douce).

176. *Fire-new.* Brand-new, fresh from the mint. Cf. *Rich. III.* 1. 3. 256 : " Your fire-new stamp of honour is scarce current ;" *T. N.* iii. 2. 23 : " fire-new from the mint," etc.

179. *Duke's.* Changed by Theo. to "King's ;" but cf. i. 2. 35 and 118 below, where Armado uses it in the same blundering way. We find it even in the mouth of the princess in ii. 1. 38 below. Dogberry applies the word to the prince in *Much Ado,* iii. 5. 22. Cf. *M. N. D.* p. 125.

182. *Tharborough.* For *thirdborough,* a kind of constable. See *T. of S.* p. 125.

187. *Contempts.* Contents. Cf. *M. W.* p. 135.

191. *Having.* Possession. The early eds. have "heaven ;" corrected

by Theo. The Coll. MS. has "hearing." The Camb. editors, St., and Clarke retain "heaven." St. remarks: "The allusion may be to the representations of *heaven*, and the attendant personifications of Faith, *Hope*, etc., in the ancient pageants."

193. *Laughing.* The early eds. have "hearing;" corrected by Capell.

196. *Style.* There is an evident play on *stile;* as in iv. 1. 92 below. See also *Much Ado*, v. 2. 6. The Coll. MS. has "chime" for *climb.*

199. *Taken with the manner.* A law term = taken in the fact, or in the act. See *W. T.* p. 205, or 1 *Hen. IV.* p. 168.

203. *Form.* Bench. For the play upon the word, cf. *R. and J.* ii. 4. 36: "who stand so much on the new form that they cannot sit at ease on the old bench."

220. *But so.* Equivalent to "but so-so," which Hanmer substituted.

232. *Ycleped.* Called; an archaism put only into the mouths of Armado and Holofernes. Cf. v. 2. 593 below.

237. *Curious-knotted.* Elaborately laid out in *knots*, or interlacing beds. Cf. *Rich. II.* iii. 4. 46: "Her knots disorder'd;" and Milton, *P. L.* iv. 242: "In beds and curious knots." See the cut on p. 35.

243. *Vassal.* The Coll. MS. has "vessel." Possibly there is a play on the word.

247. *Sorted.* Associated; as in 2 *Hen. IV.* ii. 4. 162 and *Ham.* ii. 2. 274. Cf. Bacon, *Essay* 7: "Makes them sort with meane Company."

248. *With—with.* The early eds. have "which with;" corrected by Theo.

249. *Passion.* Sorrow, grieve. Cf. *T. G. of V.* iv. 4. 172: "Ariadne passioning For Theseus' perjury;" and *V. and A.* 1059: "Dumbly she passions, franticly she doteth." Cf. the noun in v. 2. 118 below.

258. *The weaker vessel.* Taken from 1 *Peter*, iii. 7 (cf. *A. Y. L.* ii. 4. 6, 2 *Hen. IV.* ii. 4. 66, and *R. and J.* i. 1. 20), as *vessel of thy law's fury* from *Romans*, ix. 22. In the latter passage Theo. changes *vessel* to "vassal."

274. *Damosel.* The folio has "damosell" here and in the next two lines, the 1st quarto "damsel." Holofernes makes it "damosella" in iv. 2. 122 below.

290. *Lay.* Stake, wager. Cf. *Hen. V.* iv. 1. 242: "lay twenty French crowns to one," etc. Capell conjectured "man's good hat."

296. *Till then, sit thee,* etc. The reading of the 1st quarto. The folio has "vntill then sit thee," etc. The Coll. MS. reads "untill then set thee."

SCENE II.—5. *Imp.* Youngling; used only by Armado, Holofernes, and Pistol. The word originally meant an offshoot or scion of a tree; thence, figuratively, offspring or child; finally becoming limited to a young devil. Johnson remarks that Lord Cromwell, in his last letter to Henry VIII., prays for *the imp his son.* Spenser in the prologue to *F. Q.* addresses Cupid as

> "most dreaded impe of highest Jove,
> Faire Venus sonne."

Cf. *F. Q.* iii. 5. 53:

> "Fayre ympes of beauty, whose bright shining beames
> Adorne the world with like to heavenly light," etc

8. *Juvenal.* Juvenile, youth; used only by Armado, Flute (*M. N. D.* iii. 1. 97), and in jest by Falstaff (2 *Hen. IV.* i. 2. 22).

11. *Senior.* The 1st quarto has "signeor," and the folio "signeur."

13. *Epitheton.* Epithet; the reading of 2d folio. The 1st folio has "apathaton," and the quarto "apethaton."

33. *Crosses love not him.* The boy plays on *crosses* as applied to coin. We have the same pun in *A. Y. L.* ii. 4. 12 and 2 *Hen. IV.* i. 2. 253 (see our ed. p. 156). *Mere*=absolute, very. See on i. 1. 146 above.

40. *A tapster.* For other allusions to the tapster's *reckoning*, or keeping account with customers, cf. 2 *Hen. IV.* i. 2. 193 and *T. and C.* i. 2. 123.

43. *Complete.* Accomplished. Cf. *Hen. VIII.* i. 2. 118: "This man so complete," etc.

52. *The dancing horse.* A famous horse of the time, often called "Bankes' horse" from his owner, who had trained him to perform many remarkable feats. Raleigh, in his *Hist. of the World*, says: " If Banks had lived in older times, he would have shamed all the inchanters in the world; for whosoever was most famous among them could never master or instruct any beast as he did his horse." Steevens quotes, among other allusions to the animal, B. J., *Every Man Out of His Humour:* " He keeps more ado with this monster than ever Bankes did with his horse;" and the same author's *Epigrams:*

> "Old Banks the jugler, our Pythagoras,
> Grave tutor to the learned horse."

In France, according to Bishop Morton, Bankes "was brought into suspition of magicke, because of the strange feates which his horse Morocco plaied at Orieance;" but Bankes having made the beast kneel down to a crucifix and kiss it, "his adversaries rested satisfied, conceiving (as it might seeme) that the divell had no power to come neare the crosse." In Rome he was less fortunate, if we may believe Reed, who says that both horse and owner were there burned by order of the Pope. According to other authorities, however, Bankes came back safe to London, and was still living in King Charles's time, a jolly vintner in Cheapside. For fuller accounts of him and his horse, see Douce's *Illustrations*, Chambers's *Book of Days*, or Halliwell's folio ed.

60. *Courtesy.* Curtsy; used by men as well as women. See *Much Ado*, p. 159.

65. *Sweet my child.* My sweet child. See Gr. 13.

82. *Green indeed is the colour of lovers.* Some say, because of its association with jealousy, "the green-eyed monster;" others, as being the colour of the *willow*, "worn of forlorn paramours" (cf. *Much Ado*, p. 169).

85. *A green wit.* Probably, as the Camb. editors remark, there is an allusion to the *green withes* with which Samson was bound. See p. 128 above (on DRAMATIS PERSONÆ).

87. *Maculate.* The reading of the 1st quarto; the other early eds. have "immaculate."

92. *Pathetical.* The Coll. MS. has "poetical."

100. *Native she doth owe.* She possesses by nature. For *owe* = own, cf. ii. 1. 6 below. Gr. 290.

103. *The King and the Beggar.* The ballad of *King Cophetua and the Beggar-maid*, which may be found in Percy's *Reliques.* For other allusions to it, see iv. 1. 64 below, *R. and J.* ii. 1. 14, and *Rich. II.* v. 3. 80.

109. *Digression.* "Going out of the right way, transgression" (Steevens). Cf. *R. of L.* 202:

> "Then my digression is so vile, so base,
> That it will live engraven in my face."

Cf. also *digressing* in *Rich. II.* v. 3. 66.

111. *Rational hind.* Perhaps Armado's fantastic way of expressing "human hind," *hind* being a beast (a deer), as well as a boor; but *rational* may be a misprint for "irrational," as Hanmer regarded it. Farmer objects to the former interpretation, that it makes Costard a *female* animal; but Steevens quotes in reply *J. C.* i. 3. 106: "He were no lion, were not Romans hinds."

115. *A light wench.* S. is fond of playing upon the different senses of *light.* Cf. *M. of V.* v. 1. 130:

> "Let me give light, but let me not be light:
> For a light wife doth make a heavy husband."

See also ii. 1. 197 and v. 2. 25 below; and for *light* = wanton, iv. 3. 380.

119. *Let him.* The folio reading; the 1st quarto has "suffer him to," and in the next line "a" for *he.*

121. *Day-woman.* Dairy-woman. See Wb.

126. *That's hereby.* "*Hereby* is used by her (as among the vulgar in some countries) to signify *as it may happen;* he takes it in the sense of *just by*" (Steevens). We have it in the latter sense in iv. 1. 9 below. The only other instance of the word in S. is in *Rich. III.* i. 4. 94.

127. *Situate.* For the form, see Gr. 342.

130. *With that face?* Steevens says: "This cant phrase has oddly lasted till the present time; and is used by people who have no more meaning annexed to it than Fielding had, who, putting it into the mouth of Beau Didapper, thinks it necessary to apologize (in a note) for its want of sense, by adding that 'it was taken verbatim from very polite conversation.'"

135. *Come, Jaquenetta, away!* Given by the quartos and the folio to "*Clo.*" (that is, *Clown,* or Costard); corrected by Theo. The next speech is given by the 1st quarto to "*Ar.,*" by the 1st folio to "*Clo.,*" and by the later folios to "*Con.*"

141. *Fellows.* D. and H. follow Capell in reading "followers."

147. *Fast and loose.* A quibbling reference to the cheating game so called. See *K. John,* p. 156, and cf. iii. 1. 97 below.

157. *Affect.* Love; as in 84 above. Cf. *Much Ado,* i. 1. 298: "Dost thou affect her?" etc.

159. *Argument.* Proof; as in *Much Ado,* ii. 3. 243, *T. N.* iii. 2. 12, etc.

161. *Familiar.* "Familiar spirit," or demon; as in 2 *Hen. VI.* iv. 7. 114: "he has a familiar under his tongue," etc. Cf. also the adjective in *Sonn.* 86. 9:

> "that affable familiar ghost
> Which nightly gulls him with intelligence."

164. *Butt-shaft.* A kind of arrow used for shooting at *butts*, or targets. Cf. *R. and J.* p. 171.

166. *The first and second cause,* etc. Alluding to the classified *causes of quarrel* in the elaborate duelling science of the time. Cf. Touchstone's ridicule of them in *A. Y. L.* v. 4. 52 fol. ; and see our ed. p. 198, note on *By the book.* As Saviolo's book, evidently alluded to here, was printed in 1594, this passage is one of the indications of the revision of the play before the publication of the 1st quarto. See p. 10 above.

167. *Passado.* A thrust in fencing. See *R. and J.* p. 171.

170. *Manager.* Changed in the Coll. MS. to "Armiger;" but *manage* is often used of *arms.* Cf. *Rich. II.* iii. 2. 118, *2 Hen. IV.* iii. 2. 292, 301, *R. and J.* i. 1. 76, etc.

171. *Sonnet.* The reading of all the early eds. changed by Hanmer to "sonneteer," by Capell to "sonneter," by the Coll. MS. to "sonnetmaker," and by D. to "sonnetist." V. and W. read "turn sonnets." *Turn sonnet* is not unlike Armado. Cf. *Much Ado,* ii. 3. 21 : "now is he turned orthography ;" where some read "orthographer " or "orthographist."

ACT II.

SCENE I.—1. *Dearest.* Best, highest. Cf. *Temp.* p. 124, note on *The dear'st o' the loss.*

2. *Who.* The reading of the quartos and 1st folio. Gr. 274.

6. *Owe.* See on i. 2. 100 above.

16. *Chapmen.* Here =sellers ; but usually =buyers, as in *T. and C.* iv. 1. 75. Johnson remarks : "*cheap* or *cheaping* was anciently the *market; chapman* therefore is *marketman.*" Cf. Wb. *Utter'd* is here used in the commercial sense of "made to pass from one hand to another." See *R. and J.* p. 212. The meaning of the passage is that the estimation of beauty depends not on the tongue of the seller, but on the eye of the buyer. Cf. *Sonn.* 102. 4 :

> "That love is merchandiz'd whose rich esteeming
> The owner's tongue doth publish everywhere."

25. *To 's seemeth.* The reading of all the early eds. ; changed by Pope to "to us seems." Cf. *W. T.* iv. 4. 65 : "friends to 's welcome," etc.

28. *Bold of.* Confident of, trusting in.

32. *Importunes.* Accented on the penult by S. Cf. *Ham.* p. 190.

39. *Lord Longaville.* The early eds. omit *Lord,* which Capell supplied.

42. *Jaques.* Always a dissyllable in S. Cf. *A. W.* p. 160. *Solemnized* is here accented on the second syllable. See Gr. 491.

45. *Well fitted in the arts.* The reading of the 2d folio ; the 1st folio and the quartos omit *the.* W. conjectures "In arts well fitted." "*Well fitted* is *well qualified*" (Johnson).

57. *Of all.* That is, by all. Gr. 170.

60. *Though he.* The 1st folio misprints "she" for *he.*

62. *And much too little,* etc. "And my report of the good I saw is

much too little *compared* to his great worthiness" (Heath). For *to*, see Gr. 187.

68. *Hour's.* A dissyllable ; as often. Gr. 480.

72. *Conceit's expositor.* The exponent of his thought. For the use of *conceit* in S., see *Rich. II.* p. 181.

82. *Competitors.* Associates, partners. See *T. N.* p. 158, or *A. and C.* p. 175.

83. *Address'd.* Prepared, ready. See *J. C.* p. 156, or *A. Y. L.* p. 200.

88. *Unpeopled.* The reading of the folios. The 1st quarto has "unpeeled," which the Camb. editors adopt.

102. *Where.* Whereas ; as often. See *Lear*, p. 179, or 1 *Hen. IV.* p. 187. Gr. 134.

105. *And sin to break it.* Hanmer changes *And* to "Not ;" but, as Johnson remarks, "the princess shows an inconvenience very frequently attending rash oaths, whether kept or broken, produce guilt."

109. *Resolve.* Answer. Cf. *T. of S.* iv. 2. 7 : "What, master, read you? First resolve me that," etc.

118. *Long of.* Owing to, because of ; as in *M. N. D.* iii. 2. 339 : "all this coil is long of you," etc. It is generally printed "long of" in the modern eds., but not in the early ones. *Along of* in this sense does not occur in S.

123. *Fair befall*, etc. Cf. *Rich. III.* i. 3. 282 : "Now fair befall thee and thy noble house !" etc. *Fair fall* in the next line is used in the same sense ; as in *K. John*, i. 1. 78, etc.

130. *Being but the one half*, etc. Cf. the reference to Monstrelet's *Chronicle*, p. 12 above.

146. *Depart.* Part. Cf. *K. John*, ii. 1. 563 : "Hath willingly departed with a part ;" and see the note in our ed. p. 150.

148. *Gelded.* Maimed ; a favourite figure with S., as Steevens notes. Cf. *W. T.* iv. 4. 623, *Rich. II.* ii. 1. 237, 1 *Hen. IV.* iii. 1. 110, etc.

167. *I will.* The reading of 1st quarto ; "would I" in the other early eds.

173. *As you.* That you. Gr. 109.

174. *Fair harbour.* As in 1st quarto ; the other early eds. have "farther" for *fair*. The Coll. MS. reads "free."

176. *Shall we.* The folios have "we shall."

179. *Lady, I will*, etc. The folios give this and the next five speeches of Biron to "Boy."

183. *Fool.* The reading of 1st quarto ; the folios have "scule" or "soul."

189. *No point.* A play on the French negative *point ;* as in v. 2. 278 below. *No point* was sometimes used as an emphatic negative. Steevens quotes *The Shoemaker's Holiday*, 1600 : "No point. Shall I betray my brother ?"

193. *What lady*, etc. Steevens remarks : "It is odd that S. should make Dumain inquire after Rosaline, who was the mistress of Biron, and neglect Katherine, who was his own. Biron behaves in the same manner. Perhaps all the ladies wore masks but the princess." That they did is evident from 123 above. D. believes that the masks have nothing

to do with the matter, and that "Katherine" should be substituted for *Rosaline* in 194, and "Rosaline" for *Katherine* in 209 below.

198. *Light in the light.* See on i. 2. 115 above.

202. *God's blessing on your beard!* "That is, mayst thou have sense and seriousness more proportionate to thy beard, the length of which suits ill with such idle catches of wit!" (Johnson).

209. *Rosaline.* The early eds. have "Katherine;" corrected by Sr.

217. *Grapple.* Like *board*, a figure taken from naval warfare. The play on *ships* and *sheeps* indicates that the words were pronounced nearly alike. We find the same quibble in *C. of E.* iv. 1. 93 (see our ed. p. 134) and *T. G. of V.* i. 1. 73.

222. *Though several they be.* A play on *several*, which meant an en-closed field in distinction from a *common.* Steevens quotes, among other examples of the word, Holinshed, *Hist. of England:* "not to take and pale in the commons, to enlarge their severalls." *Though* seems used somewhat peculiarly, and has been explained as =*since.* Cf. *T. N.* p. 145, note on *Though it be.* We prefer Staunton's explanation: "If we take both as places devoted to pasture—the one for general, the other for par-ticular use—the meaning is easy enough. Boyet asks permission to graze on her lips. 'Not so,' she answers; 'my lips, though intended for the purpose, are not for general use.'"

233. *Retire.* For the noun, cf. *K. John*, pp. 145, 146, 178.

234. *Thorough.* Used by S. interchangeably with *through.* See *M. of V.* p. 144, note on *Throughfares.*

235. *Like an agate.* For the figures cut in agates, see *Much Ado*, p. 141, or *2 Hen. IV.* p. 153.

237. *All impatient to speak and not see*, etc. "If we take *not see* to im-ply 'not see, because it is not the tongue's faculty to see,' the sentence means that his tongue hurried to his eyes that it might express what they beheld" (Clarke). A writer in the *Edin. Rev.* (Nov. 1786) explains it: "his tongue envied the quickness of his eyes, and strove to be as rapid in his utterance as they in their perception." Perhaps Johnson is right in making it ="being impatiently desirous to see as well as speak." D., after remarking that the passage has been "utterly misunderstood" by Johnson, paraphrases it thus: "His tongue, not able to endure the hav-ing merely the power of speaking without that of seeing."

240. *To feel only looking.* Apparently =to have no perception but that of looking, to have their own sense transformed to that of sight.

244. *Point you.* Direct you, suggest to you; the reading of 1st quarto. The folios have "point out."

245. *Margent.* Alluding to the practice of putting notes, etc., in the margin of books. See *M. N. D.* p. 142, or *Ham.* p. 272 (note on *Edified by the margent*).

249. *Dispos'd.* "Inclined to merriment" (Schmidt); "inclined to rath-er loose mirth, somewhat wantonly merry" (D.). Schmidt gives the word the same sense in v. 2. 468 below, and in *T. N.* ii. 3. 88. D. cites examples of it from Peele and B. and F. Boyet parries the reproof by taking the word in its ordinary meaning.

ACT III.

SCENE I.—2. *Concolinel.* Evidently a scrap of a song, but whether the beginning or the burden of it, the title or the tune, it is impossible to determine. The songs in the old plays were often omitted in the manuscripts and printed copies, being indicated, as here, by some abbreviation, or merely by a stage-direction, as "*Here they sing*" or the Latin "*Cantant.*"

4. *Festinately.* Hastily, quickly. Cf. *festinate* in *Lear*, iii. 7. 10.

6. *Master.* Not in the folios.

7. *Brawl.* A kind of dance (Fr. *branle*). "It was performed by several persons uniting hands in a circle and giving each other continual shakes, the steps changing with the time" (Douce). Steevens quotes B. J., *Time Vindicated:*

> "The Graces did them footing teach;
> And, at the old Idalian brawls,
> They danc'd your mother·down."

10. *Canary to it.* The *canary* was a lively dance. Cf. *A. W.* ii. 1. 77:

> "make you dance canary
> With spritely fire and motion."

and see our ed. p. 147.

11. *Turning up your eye.* The folio reading; the 1st quarto has "eyelids" for *eye.*

Sometime. Used by S. interchangeably with *sometimes.*

14. *Penthouse-like.* Like a *penthouse*, a porch with a sloping roof, common in the domestic architecture of the time of S. There was one on the house in which tradition says he was born. The accompanying cut is copied from an old print. For *penthouse*, cf. *Much Ado*, iii. 3. 110, and *M. of V.* ii. 6. 1.

15. *Thin-belly doublet.* Many of the modern eds. have "thin belly-doublet;" but the 1st quarto reads "thin bellies" and the folios "thin-bellie," "thinebellie," or "thin-belly." Cf. the description of the thick-bellied doublets in Stubbes's *Anatomie of Abuses*, 1583: "Their dublettes are noe lesse monstrous than the reste; For now the fashion is to haue them hang downe to the middlest of their theighes . . . beeing so harde-quilted, and stuffed, bombasted and sewed, as they can verie hardly eyther stoupe downe, or decline them selues to the grounde, soe styffe and sturdy they stand about them . . . Now, what handsomnes can be in these dubblettes whiche stand on their bellies like, . . . (so as their bellies are thicker than all their bodyes besyde) let wise men iudge; For for my parte, handsomnes in them I see none, and muche lesse profyte. . . . Certaine I am there was neuer any kinde of apparell euer inuented that could more disproportion the body of man than these Dublets with great bellies, . . . stuffed with foure, fiue or six pound of Bombast at the least." For *bombast*, as here used, see on v. 2. 771 below.

17. *After the old painting.* "It was a common trick among some of the most indolent of the ancient masters, to place the hands in the bosom or the pockets, or conceal them in some other part of the drapery, to avoid the labour of representing them, or to disguise their own want of skill to employ them with grace and propriety" (Steevens).

18. *Complements.* Changed by Hanmer to "'complishments;'" but that was a common meaning of the word. See on i. 1. 166 above.

20. *Do you note me?* Hanmer's reading. The folio has "and make them men of note: do you note men that most are affected to these?"

23. *By my penny of observation.* Alluding to the famous old piece called *A Penniworth of Wit* (Farmer). The Coll. MS. changes *penny* ("penne" in the 1st quarto and 1st folio) to "paine."

25. *The hobby-horse is forgot.* Moth follows up the "But O, but O—" with the remainder of a line in an old song bewailing the omission of the hobby-horse from the May games. Cf. *Ham.* iii. 2. 142: "or else shall he suffer not thinking on, with the hobby-horse, whose epitaph is 'For, O, for, O, the hobby-horse is forgot!'" See also B. J., *Entertainment at Althorpe:* "But see, the hobby-horse is forgot;" B. and F., *Women Pleased*, iv. 1: "Shall the hobby-horse be forgot then?" etc. This omission is said to have been due to the opposition made by the Puritans to the morris-dances of the May festivities. For a full account of these games, see Douce's *Illustrations* or Brand's *Popular Antiquities.* The *hobby-horse*, says Tollet, "is a spirited horse of pasteboard, in which the master dances and displays tricks of legerdemain." A ladle was hung from the horse's mouth for receiving money given by the lookers-on.

45. *Message.* Changed in the Coll. MS. to "messenger;" but the meaning seems to be that the foolish message is *well sympathized* (or has its appropriate counterpart) in the foolish messenger.

60. *Voluble.* The folio reading; the 1st quarto has "volable," which the Camb. ed. retains. For *free* the Coll. MS. has "fair."

61. *By thy favour*, etc. "*Welkin* is the sky, to which Armado, with the false dignity of a Spaniard, makes an apology for sighing in its face" (Johnson).

62. *Most rude.* The Coll. MS. has "moist-eyed."

64. *A costard broken*, etc. He plays on the word *costard*, which was used jocosely for head. See *Lear*, p. 248, or *Rich. III.* p. 195.

66. *No salve in them all.* The early eds. have "in thee male" or "in the male." Capell reads "in the matter," and Johnson conjectured "in the mail" (that is, in the *bag*) or "in the vale." The reading in the text was suggested by Tyrwhitt. It may be noted that *mail* is not used by S, except in *T. and C.* iii. 3. 52, where it is = armour. As Clarke says, Costard seems to take *enigma, riddle,* and *l'envoy* to be various kinds of salve. On the virtue of the *plantain* for a *broken shin*, cf. *R. and J.* i. 2. 52:

> "*Romeo.* Your plantain-leaf is excellent for that.
> *Benvolio.* For what, I pray thee?
> *Romeo.*   For your broken shin."

Broken, by the way, means bruised so as to be bloody. See *R. and J.* p. 51, note on the passage just quoted.

74. *Is not l'envoy a salve?* Some see here a pun on *salve* and the Latin *salve*, which was used sometimes as a *parting* salutation.

77. *Tofore.* Cf. *T. A.* iii. 1. 294: "as thou tofore hast been." *Sain* is Armado's rhyming "license" for *said*. The folio has "faine."

86. *Adding.* Here and in 92 below the Coll. MS. reads "making."

95. *The boy hath sold him a bargain.* "This comedy is running over with allusions to country sports—one of the many proofs that, in its original shape, it may be assigned to the author's greenest years. The sport which so delights Costard, about the fox, the ape, and the humble-bee, has been explained by Capell, whose lumbering and obscure comments upon Shakespeare have been pillaged and sneered at by the other commentators. In this instance, they take no notice of him. It seems, according to Capell, that 'selling a bargain' consisted in drawing a person in, by some stratagem, to proclaim himself fool, by his own lips; and thus, when Moth makes his master repeat the *l'envoy*, ending in the goose, he proclaims himself a goose, according to the rustic wit, which Costard calls *selling a bargain well*" (K).

97. *Fast and loose.* A cheating game. See on i. 2. 147 above.

104. *And he ended the market.* Alluding to the proverb "Three women and a goose make a market" (Steevens).

108. *No feeling of it.* Costard plays on *sensibly*, which sometimes meant *feelingly* in the literal sense. Cf. *Cor.* p. 207.

114. *Marry, Costard*, etc. The folio has "Sirra, Costard," etc. *Marry* is the conjecture of K. and is favoured by the reply. The Coll. MS. has "Sirrah Costard, marry," etc.

118. *Immured.* As in 2d folio, the earlier eds. having "emured."

121, 122. *Let me loose . . . set thee from durance.* H. adopts Brae's transposition of *let* and *set*. The Coll. MS. has "let me be loose" and "set thee free from durance." The style of Costard and Armado hardly calls for such tinkering.

125. *Ward.* Guard, preservation. For its use as a term in fencing (= posture of defence), see *Temp.* p. 122.

127. *Like the sequel.* That is, like the sequel of a story. Some have fancied an allusion to the French *sequelle*, a gang of followers.

128. *Incony.* Apparently = fine, delicate. Nares cites examples of the word from B. J., Marlowe, and others.

129-135. *O' my troth . . . nit!* In the early eds. these lines are printed in iv. 1, after line 136: " Lord, lord, how the ladies and I have put him down!" There they are evidently out of place, and St. conjectured that they belong here. H. was the first to make the transposition. There is no line rhyming to 133, and some suppose one to have been lost; but it is quite as probable, as H. suggests, that 133 is either an interpolation, or a line struck out by the poet in revising the play, but accidentally retained by the transcriber or printer. See on iv. 3. 294 below.

131. *Armado o' th' one side.* The 1st quarto has " Armatho ath toothen side," and the folio " *Armathor* ath to the side." The text is due to Rowe. W. reads " Armado o' th' to side "—"the to side" being an old expression for "the hither side."

133. *To see him*, etc. The Coll. MS. fills out the couplet with " Looking babies in her eyes his passion to declare."

135. *Pathetical.* The word has already been used by Armado in i. 2. 92 above. Just what either he or Costard means by it must be matter of conjecture. S. has it nowhere else, except in *A. Y. L.* iv. 1. 196, where it appears to be also an affectation. See our ed. p. 187. For the personal use of *nit*, cf. *T. of S.* iv. 3. 110, the only other instance of the word in S.

138. *Inkle.* Tape. Cf. *W. T.* p. 196.

150. *Good my knave.* My good boy. See on i. 2. 65 above. For *knave* = boy, servant, cf. *A. and C.* p. 207, or *M. of V.* p. 137.

172. *Humorous.* Capricious; as in *A. Y. L.* i. 2. 278, ii. 3. 8, etc. Schmidt explains it as "sad." Hanmer reads "amorous."

173. *Critic.* Carper; the only sense in S. Cf. *Sonn.* 112. 10 and *T. and C.* v. 2. 131. See also on iv. 3. 165 below.

174. *Pedant.* Pedagogue; the only meaning in S. Cf. *T. N.* iii. 2. 80: " A pedant that keeps a school i' the church," etc.

175. *Magnificent.* Pompous, boastful; used by S. only here and in i. 1. 188 above.

176. *Wimpled.* Hoodwinked, blindfolded. Cf. Spenser, *F. Q.* i. 1. 4:

> "Yet she much whiter; but the same did hide
> Under a veil that wimpled was full low;"

that is, drawn close about her face, like a *wimple*, a kind of veil. Cf. *F. Q.* i. 12. 22:

> "For she had layd her mournefull stole aside,
> And widow-like sad wimple thrown away."

See also Wb. s. v.

181. *Plackets.* Explained by some as = stomachers; by others as = petticoats, or the slit or opening in those garments. *Placket-hole* (cf. Wb.) is still used for the slit in a petticoat.

The *codpiece* was a part of the breeches in front, made very conspicuous in the olden time.

183. *Paritors.* The same as *apparitors*, officers of ecclesiastical courts whose duty it was to serve citations. Johnson says that they are put

under Cupid's government because the citations were most frequently issued for offences against chastity.

184. *A corporal of his field.* Farmer says: "Giles Clayton, in his *Martial Discipline*, 1591, has a chapter on the office and duty of a *corporal of the field.*" According to Tyrwhitt, his duties were similar to those of an aide-de-camp now.

185. *Like a tumbler's hoop.* Alluding to its being adorned with coloured ribbons.

187. *A German clock.* Clocks were then chiefly imported from Germany, and the dramatists of the time were fond of comparing the feminine "make-up" to their intricate machinery. Steevens cites, among other passages, *Westward Hoe*, 1607: "no German clock, no mathematical engine whatsoever, requires so much reparation;" and *A Mad World, my Masters*, 1608:

> "She consists of a hundred pieces,
> Much like your German clock, and near allied:
> Both are so nice they cannot go for pride."

188. *Out of frame.* Out of order; as in *Ham.* i. 2. 20: "disjoint and out of frame."

189. *Going right.* The early eds. have "aright;" corrected by Capell.

193. *Wightly.* The early eds. have "whitley" or "whitely," which some explain as = whitish, pale (D. makes it = sallow); but Rosaline was dark. It seems probable that the word was a misspelling of *wightly*, which the Camb. editors substitute, and which means nimble, sprightly. Spenser has both *wightly* and *wight* in this sense, and the latter is found in Chaucer; as in *C. T.* 14273 (Tyrwhitt's ed.): "With any yong man, were he never so wight," etc. The Coll. MS. has "witty."

195. *Do the deed.* Cf. *M. of V.* i. 3. 86: "And in the doing of the deed of kind," etc.

196. *Argus.* For other allusions to the hundred-eyed guardian of Io, see *M. of V.* v. 1. 230 and *T. and C.* i. 2. 31.

201. *Sue, and groan.* The 1st quarto and 1st folio omit *and*.

202. *Joan.* Often = a peasant, or a woman in humble life. Cf. v. 2. 908 below. See also *K. John*, i. 1. 184: "now can I make any Joan a lady."

ACT IV.

SCENE I.—1. *Was that the king*, etc. "This is just one of those touches that S. throws in, to mark the way in which a woman unconsciously betrays her growing preference for a man who loves her. The princess recognizes the horseman, though he is at such a distance that her attendant lord is unable to distinguish whether it be the king or not; and then she immediately covers her self-betrayal by the pretendedly indifferent words, *Whoe'er he was*, etc. S. in no one of his wondrous and numerous instances of insight into the human heart more marvellously manifests his magic power of perception than in his discernment of the workings of female nature; its delicacies, its subtleties, its reticences, its revelations, its innocent reserves, and its artless confessions. He, of all masculine writers, was most truly feminine in his knowledge of what passes within a woman's heart, and the multiform ways in which it expresses itself through a woman's acts, words, manner—nay even her very silence. He knew the eloquence of a look, the significance of a gesture, the interpretation of a tacit admission ; and, moreover, he knew how to convey them in his might of expression by ingenious inference " (Clarke).

10. *Stand.* Used in the technical sense of the hunter's station or hiding-place when waiting for game. See *Cymb.* p. 182. K. remarks: "Royal and noble ladies, in the days of Elizabeth, delighted in the somewhat unrefined sport of shooting deer with a cross-bow. In the 'alleys green' of Windsor or of Greenwich parks, the queen would take her stand, on an elevated platform, and, as the pricket or the buck was driven past her, would aim the death-shaft, amid the acclamations of her admiring courtiers. The ladies, it appears, were skilful enough at this sylvan butchering. Sir Francis Leake writes to the Earl of Shrewsbury— 'Your lordship has sent me a very great and fat stag, the welcomer being stricken by your right honourable lady's hand.' The practice was as old as the romances of the Middle Ages. But, in those days, the ladies were sometimes not so expert as the Countess of Shrewsbury ; for, in the history of Prince Arthur, a fair huntress wounds Sir Launcelot of the Lake, instead of the stag at which she aims."

17. *Fair.* For its use as a noun, cf. *M. N. D.* p. 130, note on *Your fair.*

18. *Good my glass.* My good glass ; referring sportively to the forester. Johnson supposed the *glass* to be " a small mirror set in gold hanging at her girdle," according to the fashion of French ladies at that time—and of English ladies also, as Stubbes tells us in his *Anatomie of Abuses :* "they must haue their looking glasses caryed with them whersoeuer they go. And good reason, for els how cold they see the deuil in them ?"

35. *That my heart means no ill.* That is, means no ill *to. That* is treated like the dative *him* in "never meant him any ill " (2 *Hen. VI.* ii. 3. 91), etc.

36. *Curst.* Shrewish. See *M. N. D.* p. 167.

Self-sovereignty. "Not a sovereignty *over,* but *in* themselves. So *self-sufficiency, self-consequence,* etc." (Mason). Schmidt takes it to be ="that self sovereignty," or that same sovereignty. Cf. Gr. 20.

37. *Praise sake.* See *Cor.* p. 231 (on *Conscience sake*), or Gr. 217, 471.

41. *The commonwealth.* That is, of the "new-modelled society " of the king and his associates (Mason). Johnson makes it ="the common people." The Var. of 1821 gives this line to the princess ; not noted in the Camb. ed.

42. *God dig-you-den.* God give you good even. See *R. and J.* p. 148 (note on *Good-den*), or *Hen. V.* p. 164 (note on *God-den*).

56. *Break up this capon.* That is, open this letter. Here *break up* is =the preceding *carve.* It is applied to opening a despatch (the "sealed-up oracle ") in *W. T.* iii. 2. 132 : "Break up the seals and read." See also *M. of V.* ii. 4. 10 : "to break up this " (a letter), and the note in our ed. p. 141.

Capon is used like *poulet* in French for a love-letter. Farmer quotes Henry IV. as saying : "My niece of Guise would please me best, notwithstanding the malicious reports that she loves *poulets* in paper better than in a fricasee."

57. *Importeth.* Concerneth.

64. *Illustrate.* Illustrious ; used again by Holofernes in v. 1. 109 below. It is often used by Chapman ; as in *Iliad*, xi. : "Illustrate Hector." For *King Cophetua*, see on i. 2. 103 above.

65. *Zenelophon.* Coll. reads "Penelophon," which is the name in the ballad.

66. *Annothanize.* The quartos and 1st folio have "annothanize," the later folios "anatomize," which many eds. follow. Either word would suit Armado well enough.

83–88. *Thus dost thou hear*, etc. These lines are appended to the letter as a quotation, and Warb. thought that they were really from some ridiculous poem of the time.

The *Nemean lion* is mentioned again in *Ham.* i. 4. 83, where *Nemean* is accented as here.

88. *Repasture.* Repast, food.

92. *Going o'er it.* For the play upon *style*, see on i. 1. 196 above. *Erewhile*=just now.

94. *Phantasime.* Fantastic ; as in v. 1. 18 below. The later folios have "phantasme," and most of the modern eds. "phantasm."

Monarcho was the name of an Italian, a fantastic character of the time, referred to by Meres, Nash, Churchyard, and other writers.

103. *Suitor.* This seems to have been pronounced *shooter*, and that is the spelling of the early eds. here. Steevens and Malone quote sundry passages from contemporary writers illustrating the old pronunciation. In *A. and C.* v. 2. 105, Pope and Malone took the "snites" or "suits" of the folio to be an error for "shoots."

104. *My continent of beauty.* Cf. *Ham.* v. 2. 115: "you shall find in him the continent of what part a gentleman would see."

109. *Your deer.* The play on *deer* and *dear* was a favourite one. Cf. *V. and A.* 231, *P. P.* 300, *M. W.* v. 5. 18, 123, *T. of S.* v. 2. 56, 1 *Hen. IV.* v. 4. 107, *Macb.* iv. 3. 206, etc.

110. *By the horns.* The much-worn joke on the horns of the cuckold.

118. *Queen Guinever.* The unfaithful queen of Arthur.

127. *Prick.* The point in the centre of the *mark*, or target.

Mete at. To measure with the eye in aiming, hence to aim at.

128. *Wide o' the bow-hand.* "A good deal to the left of the mark ; a term still retained in modern archery" (Douce). The *bow-hand* was the hand holding the bow, or the left hand.

129. *Clout.* "The white mark at which archers took their aim. The *pin* was the wooden pin that upheld it" (Steevens). See 2 *Hen. IV.* p. 176 (note on *Clapped i' the clout*) and *R. and J.* p. 170 (*The very pin*, etc.).

132. *Greasily.* Grossly.

134. *Rubbing.* A term in bowling. Cf. *Rich. II.* p. 197, note on *Rubs.*

136. *Lord, Lord*, etc. Here the early eds. (and the modern ones except II.) insert the seven lines, iii. 1. 129–135 above.

137. *Sola, sola!* Costard hears the noise of the hunters, and runs to join them, with a shout to attract their attention. Cf. *M. of V.* v. 1. 39, where Launcelot enters with the same cry.

SCENE II.—3. *Sanguis, in blood.* Changed by Capell to "in sanguis, blood." *In blood* was a term of the chase = in full vigour. Cf. 1 *Hen. VI.* iv. 2. 48: "If we be English deer, be then in blood," etc.

4. *Pomewater.* A kind of apple. Steevens quotes an old ballad: "Whose cheeks did resemble two rosting pomewaters." In *The Puritan,* "the pomewater of his eye" is = the apple of his eye.

10. *A buck of the first head.* According to *The Return from Parnassus,* 1606 (quoted by Steevens), "a buck is the first year, a fawn; the second year, a pricket; the third year, a sorrell; the fourth year, a soare; the fifth, a buck of the first head; the sixth year, a compleat buck."

17. *Unconfirmed.* Inexperienced, ignorant; as in *Much Ado,* iii. 3. 124: "That shows thou art unconfirmed."

21. *Twice-sod.* Sod, like *sodden,* is the participle of *seethe.* Cf. *R. of L.* 1592: "sod in tears," etc. *Twice-sod simplicity* = concentrated stupidity, as if boiled down.

28. *Which we,* etc. In the folio this reads: "which we taste and feeling, are for those parts," etc. Various emendations have been proposed, of which Tyrwhitt's in the text seems the best, and is adopted by the majority of recent editors.

30. *Patch.* A play on the word in its sense of fool, for which see *M. of V,* p. 142, or *M. N. D.* p. 160. Johnson says: "The meaning is, to be in a school would as ill become a *patch* as folly would become me." The Coll. MS. has "set" for *see.*

35. *Dictynna.* One of the names of Diana. The early eds. have "Dictisima" or "Dictissima" here, and "Dictima" or "Dictinna" in the next line. Steevens suggests that S. may have found the word in Golding's *Ovid:* "Dictynna garded with her traine, and proud of killing deere."

39. *Raught.* An old past tense and participle of *reach.* For its use as the former, cf. *Hen. V.* iv. 6. 21; and as the latter, *A. and C.* iv. 9. 30. The folios have "wrought" here, the 1st quarto "rought."

40. *The allusion holds in the exchange.* "The riddle is as good when I use the name of Adam as when I use the name of Cain" (Warb.). Mr. Brae takes *allusion* to be used in the strict Latin sense of "play, joke, or jest," and makes *exchange* = "the changing of the moon."

52. *Affect the letter.* "Practise alliteration" (Mason). For another satire on this affectation of the time, cf. *M. N. D.* v. 1. 145 fol.; and see our ed. p. 184.

54. *Preyful.* The 2d folio has "praysfull."

55. *Some say a sore.* For *sore,* or *soare,* as applied to a deer "of the fourth year," see on 10 above; also for *sorel* in the next line.

58. *O sore L.* The 1st quarto has "o sorell," and the folios "O sorell." The reading in the text is Capell's, and is generally adopted. The Camb. ed. has "makes fifty sores one sorel," which is plausible and perhaps favoured by the next line.

K

61. *If a talent be a claw.* The play on *talent* and *talon* is obvious. The latter word was sometimes written *talent.* Malone cites, among other instances, Marlowe's *Tamburlaine*, 1590:

> "and now doth ghastly death
> With greedy tallents gripe my bleeding heart."

Claw was sometimes =humour, flatter. Cf. *Much Ado*, i. 3. 18: "claw no man in his humour ;" and see our ed. p. 126.

67. *Pia mater.* The membrane covering the brain, used for the brain itself; as in *T. N.* i. 5. 123 and *T. and C.* ii. 1. 77. Here the early eds. have "primater ;" corrected by Rowe.

Upon the mellowing of occasion. At "the very riping of the time " (*M. of V.* ii. 8. 40), or when the fit occasion comes.

78. *Person.* "Parson" (the reading of the 2d folio). Steevens quotes Holinshed: "Jerom was vicar of Stepnie, and Garrard was person of Honielane," etc. St. adds from Selden, *Table Talk:* "Though we write *Parson* differently, yet 't is but *Person ;* that is, the individual Person set apart for the service of the Church, and 't is in Latin *Persona*, and *Personatus* is a *Personage*." For the play on *fierce* (which was perhaps pronounced *perse*), cf. 1 *Hen. IV.* p. 201, note on *I 'll pierce him.*

90. *Mantuan.* Giovanni Battista Spagnuoli (or Spagnoli), named *Mantuanus* from his birthplace, who died in 1516, was the author of certain *Eclogues* which the pedants of that day preferred to Virgil's, and which were read in schools. The 1st Eclogue begins with the passage quoted by Holofernes. Malone quotes references to Mantuanus from Nash and Drayton. A translation of his Latin poems by George Turbervile was printed in 1567.

92. *Venetia*, etc. In the folio this reads : "*vemchie, vencha, que non te vnde, que non te perreche*," which exactly follows the 1st quarto. The text is taken by the Camb. editors from Florio's *Second Frutes*, 1591, whence the poet probably got it. There it has the second line, " Ma chi te vede, ben gli costa." In Howel's *Letters*, it appears with a translation, thus :

> "Venetia, Venetia, chi non te vede, non te pregia,
> Ma chi t' ha troppo veduto te dispregia.
>
> Venice, Venice, none thee unseen can prize ;
> Who thee hath seen too much, will thee despise."

It is usually printed in the form in which Theo. gives it :

> "Vinegia, Vinegia,
> Chi non te vede, ei non te pregia."

101. *If love*, etc. This sonnet appears, with a few verbal variations, in *P. P.* v. See p. 11 above.

105. *Bias.* Originally a term in bowling. See *Ham.* p. 200 (on *Assays of bias*), or *T. of S.* p. 167 (on *Against the bias*).

111. *Thy voice*, etc. Malone compares *A. and C.* v. 2. 83 :

> "his voice was propertied
> As all the tuned spheres, and that to friends ;
> But when he meant to quail and shake the orb,
> He was as rattling thunder."

115. *You find not the apostrophas.* K. understands this to refer to the

apostrophes in *vow'd* and *bow'd* (" _ and 104 above), and therefore prints these "vowed" and "bowed."

116–122. *Here are only*, etc. The early eds. give this to Nathaniel; corrected by Theo.

120. *Imitari.* To imitate. The early eds. have "imitarie," with no point before it, and the Coll. MS. reads "imitating."

121. *The tired horse.* The early eds. have "tyred" for *tired.* Theo. reads "try'd," and Capell "'tired." Heath conjectures "trained." It is probably another allusion to Bankes's horse (see on i. 2. 52 above), as Farmer explains it; *tired* being ="adorned with ribbons."

123. *Ay, sir, from one Monsieur Biron.* "S. forgot himself in this passage. Jaquenetta knew nothing of Biron, and had said just before that the letter had been sent to her from Don Armado and given to her by Costard" (Mason).

133. *Royal.* The word is only in the 1st quarto.

134. *Stay not thy compliment; I forgive thy duty.* That is, do not tarry to make any formal obeisance; I excuse you from that. Cf. *M. N. D.* iv. 1. 21 : "Pray you, leave your courtesy, good mounsieur."

141. *Colourable colours.* "That is, specious or fair-seeming appearances" (Johnson); or "false pretexts" (Schmidt).

146. *Before repast.* The folios have "being" for the *before* of 1st quarto.

149. *Ben venuto.* Welcome (Italian). Cf. *T. of S.* p. 141. The folio has "bien vonuto," and the Camb. editors conjecture "bien venu too."

154. *Certes.* Certainly. Cf. *Temp.* iii. 3. 30, *C. of E.* iv. 4. 78, etc. Schmidt considers it monosyllabic in *Hen. VIII.* i. 1. 48 and *Oth.* i. 1. 16.

156. *Pauca verba.* Few words (Latin).

SCENE III.—2. *Pitched a toil.* Set a net. *Toiling in a pitch* alludes to Rosaline's complexion (Johnson).

3. *Set thee down, sorrow!* A proverbial expression. Cf. i. 1. 296 above.

5. *And ay the fool.* The folio has " I " for *ay,* as regularly, and the editors generally take it for the personal pronoun. The *ay* is the correction of W., and *ay the fool*="confirm the fool in what he said," or say *ay* to him. In the next line the common reading is "I a sheep ;" also corrected by W.

6. *It kills sheep.* Alluding to the story that Ajax, when the arms of Hector were adjudged to Ulysses instead of himself, slew a whole flock of sheep, which, in his insane fury, he mistook for the sons of Atreus.

10. *Lie in my throat.* A common expression. See *2 Hen. IV.* p. 154, note on *I had lied in my throat.*

16. *If the other three were in.* That is, in the same predicament with himself.

17. *Gets up into a tree.* The old stage-direction is "*He stands aside ;*" which was all that the humble scenic arrangements of that day could afford ; but it is evident from 74 below that Biron is meant to be above the others.

20. *Bird-bolt.* A blunt-headed arrow, used to kill birds without piercing them. Cf. *Much Ado,* i. 1. 42 and *T. N.* i. 5. 100.

25. *The night of dew.* The dewy night, the tears of sorrow. The lady's *eye-beams* are the morning sunshine on these dew-drops of his grief. Cf. *V. and A.* 481 fol.

28. *As doth thy face,* etc. Malone compares *V. and A.* 491 :

> " But hers, which through the crystal tears gave light,
> Shone like the moon in water seen by night."

31. *Triumphing.* Accented on the second syllable ; as in *R. of L.* 1388, 1 *Hen. IV.* v. 3. 15, v. 4. 14, *Rich. III.* iii. 4. 91, iv. 4. 59, etc.

36. *Dost thou.* The Coll. MS. has " thou dost."

43. *Perjure.* Perjurer. "The punishment of perjury is to wear on the breast a paper expressing the crime " (Johnson). Steevens quotes several references to the penalty.

48. *Triumviry.* The early eds. have " triumphery " or " triumphry." Rowe (1st ed.) reads " triumvirate."

49. *Love's Tyburn.* " The gallows at Tyburn was of triangular form " (Clarke).

53. *Guards.* Facings, trimmings. Cf. *Much Ado,* i. 1. 289 : " the guards are but slightly basted on ;" and see our ed. p. 124. For *hose* = breeches, see *A. Y. L.* p. 158.

54. *Slop.* The old eds. have " shop ;" corrected by Theo. *Slops* were large loose trowsers. See *Much Ado,* p. 143.

55. *Did not the heavenly rhetoric,* etc. This sonnet also appears in *P. P.* iii. A comparison of the two versions will show some slight verbal differences.

68. *To lose an oath.* By losing an oath. For the "indefinite use " of the infinitive, see Gr. 356.

69. *The liver-vein.* For the liver as the seat of love, see *A. Y. L.* p. 179.

73. *All hid, all hid.* " The children's cry at *hide and seek*" (Musgrave).

76. *More sacks to the mill !* The name of a boyish sport.

77. *Woodcocks.* The bird was supposed to have no brains, and hence was a common metaphor for a fool. See *Ham.* pp. 191, 275.

81. *She is not, corporal.* Theo. reads "is but corporal," and the Coll. MS. "is most corporal ;" but there is no absolute necessity for any change. As Clarke remarks, Biron styles Dumain *corporal* as he has before called himself " a *corporal* of his (Love's) field," with perhaps an allusion to the word *mortal* just used by Dumain. K., V., St., the Camb. editors, W. and others retain the old text.

82. *Quoted.* Noted, marked. Cf. *K. John,* iv. 2. 222 :

> " A fellow by the hand of nature mark'd,
> Quoted and sign'd to do a deed of shame," etc.

See also v. 2. 776 below. In the early eds. the word is spelt " coted," as it was pronounced.

The meaning is that " amber itself is regarded as foul when compared with her hair " (Mason).

91. *Reigns in my blood.* For the figure, cf. *Ham.* iv. 3. 68 : " For like the hectic in my blood he rages."

92. *Incision.* Blood-letting; the only sense in S. Cf. *M. of V.* ii. 1. 6, *A. Y. L.* iii. 2. 75, *Rich. II.* i. 1. 155, *Hen. V.* iv. 2. 9, etc.

93. *Misprision.* Mistake, misapprehension. See *M. N. D.* p. 162.

96. *On a day*, etc. This poem is in *P. P.* xvii., and also in *England's Helicon*, 1614.

101. *Can passage find.* In the *P. P.* we find "gan" for *can*. The latter is an old spelling of *gan*. Cf. Spenser, *F. Q.* i. 4. 46: "With gentle words he can her fayrely greet," etc. See also Wb.

102. *That.* So that; as in v. 2. 9 below. Gr. 283.

103. *Wish'd.* The reading in *P. P.* and the 2d folio; the quartos and 1st folio have "wish."

106. *Is sworn.* "Hath sworn" in *P. P.* and *England's Helicon*.

107. *Thorn.* "Throne" in the early eds. and *P. P.;* corrected by Rowe from *England's Helicon*.

112. *Thou for whom*, etc. The reading of all the early versions. Rowe reads "even Jove," and the Coll. MS. "great Jove."

117. *Fasting.* Hungry, longing; changed by Capell to "lasting." Theo. conjectured "festering."

126. *You blush.* Changed by the Coll. MS. to "blush you." H. adopts Walker's conjecture of "your blush."

130. *Wreathed.* Folded. Cf. *T. G. of V.* ii. 1. 19: "to wreathe your arms," etc.

137. *One, her.* The 2d folio drops *One*, and Walker conjectures "One's."

140. *When that.* For *that* as a "conjunctional affix," see Gr. 287.

141. *Faith so infringed*, etc. The *so* (the reading of the Globe ed.) is not in the folio. The 2d folio has "A faith." D. and H. adopt Walker's conjecture "Of faith." "Such faith" has also been proposed. In the 1st quarto the line is at the top of the page, and the catch-word at the bottom of the preceding page is "Fayth," showing, as the Camb. editors remark, that the omitted word, whatever it may be, was not the first in the line.

145. *Know so much by me.* That is, about me. Cf. *A. W.* v. 3. 237: "By him and by this woman here what know you?" See also 1 *Cor.* iv. 4: "I know nothing by myself" (that is, against myself). Gr. 145.

146. *Advancing.* W. has "*Descends*," and remarks: "The original has no stage-direction here. It is noteworthy that Biron does not say 'Now I *descend*,' but 'Now *step I forth*,' which betrays the poet's consciousness that, although he imagined the character to be in a tree, the actor who played it would be on the same plane with the others." We are inclined, however, to think that "*Advancing*" is the proper stage-direction, and that *step I forth* refers to his coming forward *after* descending from the tree. What the stage usage is we are unable to say.

150. *Coaches; in*, etc. The early eds. have "couches in," etc.; corrected by Hanmer. Cf. 30 above.

153. *Like of.* See on i. 1. 107 above.

156. *Mote . . . mote.* The early eds. have "moth . . . moth." Cf. p. 128 above.

159. *Teen.* Grief, pain. Cf. *Temp.* i. 2. 64: "To think o' the teen that I have turn'd you to;" and see our ed. p. 113.

161. *Gnat.* Schmidt compares *Per.* ii. 3. 62: "And princes not doing so are like to gnats." Theo. reads "knot," and Johnson conjectures "sot." Mason says: "Biron is abusing the king for his sonneting like a minstrel, and compares him to a *gnat,* which always sings as it flies." From the context it is quite as likely that *gnat* is simply a hit at the king for "coming down" to such petty business as love-making.

162. *Gig.* A kind of top. Cf. v. 1. 60, 62 below. S. uses the word nowhere else.

163. *Profound.* Accented on the first syllable because coming before a noun accented on the first syllable. Cf. *Ham.* iv. 1. 1: "There's matter in these sighs, these profound heaves." See, on the other hand, v. 2. 52 below, or *Sonn.* 112. 9. See also on i. 1. 134 above.

164. *Push-pin.* A child's game.

165. *Critic Timon.* Cynical Timon. See on iii. 1. 173 above. S. uses the adjective only here, but we have *critical*=censorious, in *M. N. D.* v. 1. 54 and *Oth.* ii. 1. 120 (the only instances of the word).

169. *A caudle, ho!* A *caudle* was a warm, cordial drink, often used for the sick. The folios misprint "candle" (the 1st quarto has *caudle*), as in 2 *Hen. VI.* iv. 7. 95, the only other instance of the noun in S.

171. *To me ... by you.* The early eds. have "by me ... to you;" corrected by Capell.

175. *Men like you,* etc. The quartos and 1st folio have "men like men of inconstancy;" corrected by D. (Walker's conjecture). Various other emendations not worthy of note have been suggested.

177. *Love.* The reading of 1st quarto (Duke of Devonshire's copy); other copies having "Ione." The other early eds. have "Ioane" or "Joan;" and some modern eds. read "Joan." See on iii. 1. 202 above.

178. *Pruning me.* Adorning myself. See 1 *Hen. IV.* p. 142.

180. *State.* Mode of *standing,* as opposed to *gait;* attitude. Cf. *station* in *Ham.* iii. 4. 58 and *A. and C.* iii. 3. 22.

182. *True man.* Often opposed to *thief.* See 1 *Hen. IV.* p. 168, or *Cymb.* p. 182.

184. *Present.* Document to be *presented.* Some see an allusion to the legal formula "Be it known to all men by these presents;" but this seems unnecessary. Sr. reads "presentment," and the Coll. MS. has "peasant."

185. *Makes.* Does. Cf. *A. Y. L.* i. 1. 31: "what make you here?" This use of the word was very common, and is played upon, as here, in *Rich. III.* i. 3. 164 fol.

189. *Person.* Parson; the reading of the early eds. See on iv. 2. 78 above.

196. *Toy.* Trifle; as in 165 above. Cf. 1 *Hen. VI.* iv. 1. 145: "a toy, a thing of no regard," etc.

202. *Mess.* Sometimes =a party of *four,* as "at great dinners the company was usually arranged into fours" (Nares). Cf. v. 2. 363 below, and see also 3 *Hen. VI.* i. 4. 73: "your mess of sons."

207. *Turtles.* Turtle-doves; the only sense in S. Cf. v. 2. 893 below, See also *W. T.* p. 194.

211. *Show.* The folios have "will shew."

214. *Of all hands.* "At any rate, in any case" (Schmidt). Clarke makes it ="on all sides, on every account."

218. *Gorgeous east.* Milton has adopted this in *P. L.* ii. 3 : "Or where the gorgeous east with richest hand," etc.

219. *Strucken.* The early eds. have "strooken." Cf. Gr. 344.

235. *To things of sale*, etc. Malone quotes *Sonn.* 21. 14 : "I will not praise that purpose not to sell."

243. *Wood.* The early eds. have " word;" corrected by Rowe (1st ed.).

248. *No face*, etc. Cf. *Sonn.* 132. 13 :

> "Then will I swear beauty herself is black,
>   And all they foul that thy complexion lack."

See also *Sonn.* 127.

250. *Shade.* The early eds. have "schoole" or "school." Warb. conjectures "scowl," Theo. "stole," Thirlby "soul," D. "soil," Halliwell "scroll," "shroud," or " seal," and the Camb. editors "suit." *Shade* is from the Coll. MS. and is adopted by W. and H.

251. *And beauty's crest*, etc. " *Crest* is here properly opposed to *badge*. *Black*, says the king, is the *badge of hell*, but that which graces the heaven is the *crest of beauty*. *Black* darkens hell, and is therefore hateful; *white* adorns heaven, and is therefore lovely" (Johnson). Tollet says: "In heraldry, a *crest* is a device placed above a coat of arms. S. therefore uses it in a sense equivalent to *top* or *utmost height*." Cf. *K. John*, iv. 3. 46. For *crest*, Hanmer reads "dress," and the Coll. MS. "best."

254. *Usurping hair.* On Shakespeare's repugnance to false hair, see *M. of V.* p. 149, note on *The dowry*, etc. For his allusions to *painting*, cf. *M. for M.* iii. 2. 83, iv. 2. 40, *T. of A.* iv. 3. 147, *Ham.* v. 1. 213, *W. T.* iv. 4. 101, etc. Hanmer has "usurped." The 1st folio omits *and*, and the 2d and 3d folios have "an."

263. *Crack.* Boast. Cf. *Cymb.* v. 5. 177:

> "our brags
> Were crack'd of kitchen-trulls."

The 1st quarto and 1st and 2d folios have " crake."

283. *Quillets.* Casuistries, subtleties, nice distinctions of logic or law. Cf. 1 *Hen. VI.* ii. 4. 17 : "these nice sharp quillets of the law ;" *Ham.* v. 1. 108: "his quiddits now, his quillets," etc.

292. *Book.* Some editors put a colon or semicolon after this word.

294-299. *For when . . . fire.* These lines are evidently a part of the first sketch of the play accidentally retained in the revision. They are repeated in new form below. The same is true of 307-314 below. D. and H. strike out both passages.

300. *Poisons up.* For the intensive use of *up*, cf. "kill them up" in *A. Y. L.* ii. 1. 62, and see our ed. p. 155. See also *flatter up* in v. 2. 804 below. Most editors (except St.) follow Theo. in reading "prisons up;" but the simile which follows seems to favour the old text. There is a closer analogy between *poisoning* and *tiring* than between *prisoning* and *tiring*. The early eds. all have "poysons." The Camb. editors, after adopting " prisons," return to *poisons* in the Globe ed.

308. *Teaches such beauty*, etc. "That is, a lady's eyes give a fuller no-

tion of *beauty* than any author " (Johnson). Warb. reads "duty," and the Coll. MS. "learning."

311. *Then when*, etc. After this line, the quartos and 1st folio insert the imperfect line " With our selues."

314. *Our books.* "That is, our *true* books, from which we derive most information—the *eyes* of women " (Malone).

317. *Numbers.* "Poetical measures " (Johnson) ; changed by Hanmer to "notions."

331. *When the suspicious head of theft is stopp'd.* " That is, a lover in pursuit of his mistress has his sense of hearing quicker than a *thief* (who suspects every sound he hears) in pursuit of his prey "(Warb.).

332. *Sensible.* Sensitive ; as in *Temp.* ii. 1. 174 : "sensible and nimble lungs," etc.

336. *Valour.* Theo. reads "savour," and "flavour" has been conjectured. The reference is of course to the daring of Hercules in attempting to get the golden apples. *Hesperides* is used for the Gardens of the Hesperides. Cf. *Per.* i. 1. 27 :

> "Before thee stands this fair Hesperides,
> With golden fruit, but dangerous to be touch'd ;
> For death-like dragons here affright thee hard."

Malone quotes Greene's *Friar Bacon*, etc., 1598 : " That watch'd the garden call'd Hesperides."

339. *Voice.* H. prints " voice'." Possibly the word is a plural, like *sense* in *Sonn.* 112. 10, etc. See Gr. 471. The plural verb may, however, be explained as an instance of " confusion of proximity " Gr. 412). Abbott is doubtful under which head to put the passage. Hanmer reads "Makes" for *Make*.

The meaning of the passage may be, " When love speaks, the accordant voice of all the gods makes heaven drowsy with the harmony " (Clarke) ; or, as we are inclined to think, when love speaks, it is *like* the voices of all the gods blended in soul-soothing harmony.

353. *A word that loves all men.* Malone thinks this means "that is pleasing to all men," and compares the *impersonal* use of " it likes me " =it pleases me. Of course there is no analogy whatever between the two. The expression was used for the sake of the antithesis, and probably with a somewhat loose reference to the idea that love affects all men, or, possibly, is a blessing to all men. Hanmer reads "that moves all men," and Warb. " all women love." Heath conjectures " joys " for *loves*, and Mason "leads."

364. *Get the sun of them.* As Malone notes, it was an advantage in the days of archery to have the sun at the back of the bowmen and in the face of the enemy ; as Henry V. found at the battle of Agincourt.

365. *Glozes.* Sophistries, special pleadings ; the only instance of the noun in S. For the verb, see *Hen. V.* p. 146.

375. *Love.* Venus. Cf. *C. of E.* p. 128.

377. *Be time.* That is, be sufficient time (Clarke). The reading of the early eds. changed by Rowe to " betime," which Schmidt regards as a verb ="betide, chance."

378. *Allons! allons!* The early eds. have "Alone, alone;" corrected by Theo. (the conjecture of Warb.). See on v. 1. 137 below.

Sow'd cockle reap'd no corn. "This proverbial expression intimates that, beginning with perjury, they can expect to reap nothing but falsehood" (Warb.).

ACT V.

SCENE I.—1. *Satis quod sufficit.* "Enough 's as good as a feast" (Steevens).

2. *Reasons.* Arguments; or, perhaps, as Johnson and others explain it, "discourse, conversation."

4. *Affection.* "Affectation" (2d folio). In *Ham.* ii. 2. 464, the quartos have "affection," the folios "affectation." See also on v. 2. 409 below. *Affectioned* (=affected) occurs in *T. N.* ii. 3. 160.

5. *Opinion.* Dogmatism; or, perhaps, self-conceit. Cf. 1 *Hen. IV.* p. 175.

9. *Novi hominem tanquam te.* I know the man as well as I do you.

10. *His tongue filed.* His speech is polished or refined. Cf. *Sonn.* 85. 4: "And precious phrase by all the Muses fil'd," etc.

12. *Thrasonical.* Boastful; like Thraso in Terence's *Eunuchus.* Cf. *A. Y. L.* p. 193.

Picked. Over-refined, fastidious. Cf. *Ham.* v. 1. 151: "the age is grown so picked;" and *K. John,* i. 1. 193: "My picked man of countries." Travellers were much given to this affectation; which explains *peregrinate* here.

18. *Phantasimes.* Fantastics. See on iv. 1. 94 above.

Point-device = finical, "up to the best mark devisable;" as in *A. Y. L.* iii. 2. 401: "you are rather point-device in your accoutrements." For *companions* used contemptuously (=fellows), see *Temp.* p. 131, note on *Your fellow.*

19. *Rackers of orthography,* etc. W. remarks: "This passage has especial interest on account of its testimony to the condition of our language when it was written. In his pedagoguish wrath, the Pedant lets us know that consonants now silent were then heard on the lips of purists, that compound words preserved the forms and sounds of their elements, and that vowels were pronounced more purely and openly than they now are. The change from the ancient to what may be called the modern pronunciation appears to have begun, among the more cultivated classes, just before S. commenced his career, and to have been completed in the course of about fifty years—that is, from about 1575 to about 1625 . . . With regard to the completion of this change, the following passages from Charles Butler's *English Grammar,* Oxford, 1633, are decisive: 'Another use of the letters is to show the derivation of a word: namely, when we keep a letter in the derivative, &c. . . . also when a letter not sounded in the English is yet written, because it is in the language from which the word came: as *b* in *debt, doubt; e* in *George; g* in *deseign, flegme, reign, signe; h* in *Thomas, authoriti; l* in *salve,* &c.

... *L* after *a* and before *f, v, k,* or *m* is vulgarly sounded like *u* (or, with the *a,* like the diphthong *au*) ; before *f* as in *calf, half ;* before *v* as in *salv, calvs, halvs,* etc.' "

23. *Abhominable.* The old spelling, and evidently also the pronunciation, of the word.

Insinuateth me. Intimates or suggests to me. Hanmer reads "to me," and the Coll. MS. "one" for *me.*

24. For *insanire* the early eds. have "infamie," for which Theo. reads "insanie," Warb. "insanity," and the Coll. MS. "insania." *Insanire,* which is favoured by the use of the infinitive in defining it, was suggested by Walker.

Ne intelligis? Do you understand? Johnson conjectures "nonne" for *ne.*

26. *Laus Deo,* etc. The folio reads here :

> "*Cura.   Laus Deo, bene intelligo.*
> *Peda.   Bome boon for boon prescian,* a little scratcht, 'twil serue."

The reading in the text is due to Theo., who says : "The curate, addressing with complaisance his brother pedant, says *bone* to him, as we frequently in Terence find *bone vir ;* but the pedant, thinking he had mistaken the adverb, thus descants on it : '*Bone—bone for bene :* Priscian a little scratched : 't will serve.' Alluding to the common phrase, *Diminuis Prisciani caput,* applied to such as speak false Latin." This is ingenious, but we have our doubts whether it is anything more than a plausible mending of a hopelessly corrupt passage. It is, however, much to be preferred to the modification of it in the modern editions that have adopted it. These, without exception (at least, so far as we are aware), read "bone intelligo," making Nathaniel actually wrong in the use of the adverb. It is hardly conceivable that he should be guilty of a blunder for which a schoolboy ought to be whipped ; and besides he has used the correct form in "omne bene," in iv. 2. 31 above—a fact which all the editors appear to have overlooked. It is certainly more reasonable to suppose, as Theo. does, that Nathaniel's *bone* is the vocative of the adjective, and that Holofernes takes it to be a slip for the adverb ; which is natural enough, as *bene intelligo* is a common phrase. Being a pedagogue, and used to hearing such blunders from his pupils, it does not occur to him that Nathaniel would not be likely to make them.

The Camb. editors (followed by H.) retain the *bene intelligo,* and make Holofernes reply : " Bon, bon, fort bon, Priscian ! a little scratched ; 't will serve." They say : " Holofernes patronizingly calls Sir Nathaniel *Priscian,* but, pedagogue-like, will not admit his perfect accuracy." It seems improbable, however, that he would play the critic in a case like this, where the construction is so simple that no possible question could be raised about it. Besides, the pedant does not elsewhere quote French, and Latin might naturally be expected from him here.

29. *Videsne quis venit?* Do you see who is coming?

30. *Video, et gaudeo.* I see, and rejoice.

37. *Alms-basket of words.* The refuse of words. As Malone notes, the refuse meat of families was put into a basket and given to the poor. He cites Florio's *Second Frutes,* 1591 : "Take away the table, fould up

the cloth, and put all these pieces of broken meat into a basket for the poor."

39. *Honorificabilitudinitatibus.* "This word, whencesoever it comes, is often mentioned as the longest word known" (Johnson).

40. *Flap-dragon.* "Some small combustible body, fired at one end, and put afloat in a glass of liquor" (Johnson). Cf. 2 *Hen. IV.* ii. 4. 267 : "drinks off candle-ends for flap-dragons." Almonds, plums, or raisins were commonly used for the purpose.

43. *Horn-book.* The child's primer, the pages of which were covered with thin horn, to keep them from being soiled or torn. S. uses the word only here.

45. *Pueritia.* Literally, boyhood ; used affectedly for *puer,* boy.

48. *Quis.* Who.

50. *The fifth, if I.* K. says : "The pedant asks who is the silly sheep —quis, quis? 'The third of the five vowels if you repeat them,' says Moth ; and the pedant does repeat them—a, e, I ; the other two clinches it, says Moth, o, u (O you). This may appear a poor conundrum, and a low conceit, as Theobald has it, but the satire is in opposing the pedantry of the boy to the pedantry of the man, and making the pedant have the worst of it in what he calls 'a quick venew of wit.'"

53. *Longaville.* Here rhyming with *mile,* as above (iv. 3. 128) with *compile.* Cf. p. 128 above.

54. *Venue.* Touch, hit ; a fencing term. It is the same as *veney* in *M. W.* i. 1. 296. See our ed. p. 135.

55. *Home.* That is, a home thrust. Cf. v. 2. 628 below.

56. *Wit-old.* A play upon *wittol* (=cuckold), for which see *M. W.* p. 148.

62. *Circum circa.* That is, round and round.

71. *Preambulate.* The early eds. have "preambulat," for which Theo. reads "præambula." *Preambulate* is from the Camb. ed.

72. *Charge-house.* A word not found elsewhere, and possibly a corruption. Steevens thought it might be ="a free school" (apparently on the *lucus a non lucendo* principle), but it is more likely one at which a fee was charged. Theo. conjectures "church-house," and the Coll. MS. has "large house." Capell takes it to be a corruption of *Charter-house,* as that word is of *Chartreuse.* This is not improbable. H. reads "Chartreuse ;" but, even if that is the meaning, the corruption may have been put intentionally into the mouth of Armado.

83. *Choice.* The quartos and 1st folio have "chose," the 2d folio "choise," and the other folios "choice."

86. *Inward.* Confidential, private. Cf. *Rich. III.* iii. 4. 8 : "Who is most inward with the royal duke?" See also the noun in *M. for M.* iii. 2. 138.

87. *Remember thy courtesy.* This was a phrase of the time, bidding a person who had taken off his hat as an act of courtesy, to put it on again. See *Ham.* p. 270. Dr. Ingleby (*Shakes. Hermeneutics,* p. 74) is probably right in his explanation of the origin of the phrase : "It arose, we think, as follows : the *courtesy* was the temporary removal of the hat from the head, and that was finished as soon as the hat was replaced. If any one

from ill-breeding or over-politeness stood uncovered for a longer time than was necessary to perform the simple act of courtesy, the person so saluted reminded him of the fact that the removal of the hat was a courtesy : and this was expressed by the euphemism 'Remember thy courtesy,' which thus implied 'Complete your courtesy, and replace your hat.'"

89. *Importunate.* The folio reading. The 1st quarto has "importunt," and the Camb. ed. "important."

93. *Excrement.* The word is applied to the hair or beard in five out of six passages in which S. uses it. See *Ham.* p. 238.

99. *Chuck.* A term of endearment. See *Macb.* p. 212.

100. *Antique.* The early eds. use *antique* and *antick* indiscriminately, but with the accent always on the first syllable. Cf. *A. Y. L.* p. 152, or *Macb.* p. 234. See also 132 below.

105. *The Nine Worthies.* Famous personages, often alluded to, and classed somewhat arbitrarily, like the Seven Wonders of the World. They were commonly said to be three Gentiles—Hector, Alexander, Julius Cæsar; three Jews—Joshua, David, Judas Maccabæus; and three Christians—Arthur, Charlemagne, Godfrey of Bouillon. In the present play we find Pompey and Hercules among the number. Cf. 2 *Hen. IV.* ii. 4. 238: "ten times better than the Nine Worthies.

106. *Sir Nathaniel.* The early eds. have "Sir Holofernes;" corrected by Capell.

113. *Myself or.* The early eds. have "myself and ;" corrected by Capell. The passage is probably otherwise corrupt.

115. *Pass.* Pass as, represent.

120. *Present.* Represent ; as in *Temp.* iv. 1. 167 : "When I presented Ceres," etc. See also many instances of the word below.

125. *Make an offence gracious.* "Convert an offence against yourselves into a dramatic propriety" (Steevens).

132. *Fadge.* Suit, or turn out well ; as in *T. N.* ii. 2. 34 : "How will this fadge?"

134. *Via.* Away (Italian) ; used as "an adverb of encouragement" (Florio).

137. *Allons.* The early eds. have "Alone," as in iv. 3. 378 above.

139. *The hay.* Some say that to *dance the hay* was to dance in a ring ; others that *hay* was the name of a country-dance.

SCENE II.—2. *Fairings.* Presents (originally, those bought at a fair) ; used by S. only here.

3. *A lady*, etc. Walker conjectures that this line and the next should be transposed ; but it is not an unnatural exclamation as it stands.

10. *Wax.* Grow ; with an obvious play on the noun.

12. *Shrewd.* Mischievous, evil ; the original sense of the word. See *Hen. VIII.* p. 202. *Unhappy* seems to be =roguish ; as in *A. W.* iv. 5. 66 : "A shrewd knave and an unhappy." See our ed. p. 174. *Gallows* =one who deserves the gallows.

19. *Mouse.* Cf. *Ham.* iii. 4. 183 : "call you his mouse." See also *T. N.* i. 5. 69.

22. *Taking it in snuff.* A play on the sense of taking it ill, or being

vexed at it. Cf. Hotspur's quibble in 1 *Hen. IV.* i. 3. 41. See also *M. N. D.* v. 1. 254.

28. *Past cure is still past care.* The early eds. transpose *cure* and *care* ; corrected by Theo. For the proverb, cf. *Sonn.* 147. 9 : " Past cure I am, now reason is past care." See also *R. and J.* p. 200, note on *Cure.*

29. *Bandied.* Like *set* (=game), an allusion to tennis. Cf. *K. John,* v. 2. 107 and *Hen. V.* i. 2. 262. See also *R. and J.* ii. 5. 114.

33. *Favour.* Playing upon its sense of *face.* Cf. iv. 3. 257 above.

43. *Ware pencils.* Beware of pencils. *Ware* is not a contraction of *beware,* as generally printed. Cf. Wb.

" Rosaline says that Biron had drawn her picture in his letter ; and afterwards playing on the word *letter,* Katherine compares her to a text B. Rosaline in reply advises her to beware of pencils, that is, of drawing likenesses, lest she should retaliate ; which she afterwards does by comparing her to a red dominical letter, and calling her marks of the small-pox *O's* " (Mason). In the old calendars (as in some modern ones) the *dominical* letter denoting Sunday was printed in red.

45. *Not so.* Found in the 1st quarto, but not in the other early eds.

46. *A pox of that jest !* Theo. considered this rather coarse in the mouth of a princess ; but, as Farmer reminds him, only the small-pox is meant. Davison has a canzonet on his lady's "sicknesse of the poxe ;" and Dr. Donne writes to his sister : "I found Pegge had the poxe—I humbly thank God, it hath not much disfigured her."

Beshrew was a mild form of imprecation ; and *shrow* was another spelling of *shrew* (cf. *shew* and *show,* etc.), representing the pronunciation of the word. For the rhyme, cf. *T. of S.* iv. 1. 213, v. 2. 28, 188. D. omits *I* (Lettsom's conjecture), as "in 29 out of 31 examples in S. *beshrew* is a mere exclamatory imprecation." The other instance of the verb with a pronoun expressed is in *R. and J.* v. 2. 26 : " She will beshrew me much."

47. *But, Katherine,* etc. It has been conjectured that either *Katherine* should be omitted, or we should read "sent you from Dumain."

61. *In by the week.* A cant phrase of the time, sometimes =in love, as in the old *Roister Doister* (St.).

65. *Hests.* The quartos and 1st folio have "device," and the later folios "all to my behests." *Hests* (cf. *Temp.* i. 2. 274, iii. 1. 37, iv. 1. 65, and see our ed. p. 118) was suggested by Walker.

66. *And make him proud,* etc. "Make him proud to flatter me who make a mock of his flattery" (*Edin. Rev.* Nov. 1786).

67. *Potent-like.* The early eds. have "perttaunt-like" or "pertaunt-like." Theo. reads "pedant-like," Hanmer and H. "portent-like," Capell "pageant-like," the Coll. MS. "potently," and W. "persaunt-like" (=piercingly). *Potent-like* is due to Sr.

69. *Catch'd.* For the form, cf. *A. W.* i. 3. 176 and *R. and J.* iv. 5. 48. We find it as the past tense in *Cor.* i. 3. 68.

74. *Wantonness.* The quartos and 1st folio have "wantons be ;" corrected in 2d folio.

78. *Simplicity.* Silliness ; as in 52 above.

79. *Mirth is.* The folios omit *is,* which is found in the 1st quarto. In the next line the quarto misprints "stable" for *stabb'd.*

80. In *stabb'd with laughter* some see an allusion to the "stitch in the side" often caused by laughter.

82. *Encounters.* The abstract for the concrete. The Coll. MS. has "encounterers," which occurs in *T. and C.* iv. 5. 58.

87. *Saint Denis.* The patron saint of France. Cf. *Hen. V.* v. 2. 193, 220, etc. For *Saint Cupid*, cf. iv. 3. 361 above.

88. *Charge their breath against us.* Make this wordy attack upon us. The Coll. MS. spoils it by reading "charge the breach."

92. *Address.* Directed; as in *T. N.* i. 4. 15: "address thy gait unto her," etc. H. explains it as "*made ready* or *prepared.*"

101. *Made a doubt.* Expressed the fear. Cf. *Rich. II.* p. 198, note on '*T is doubt.*

104. *Audaciously.* Boldly, with confidence.

117. *Spleen ridiculous.* "Ridiculous fit of laughter" (Johnson). For *spleen*=a sudden impulse, or fit, see *M. N. D.* p. 129.

118. *Passion's solemn tears.* That is, tears which are usually the expression of deep sorrow. For *passion*, cf. *Ham.* p. 212. See also the verb in i. 1. 249 above. The 1st quarto prints "follie pashions solembe," and the folio "folly passions solemne." Pope reads "folly, passions, solemn tears," and the Coll. MS. has "sudden" for *solemn.* St. conjectures "folly's passion, solemn tears."

121. *Like Muscovites or Russians.* K. remarks: "For the Russian or Muscovite habits assumed by the king and nobles of Navarre, we are indebted to Vecellio. At page 303 of the edition of 1598, we find a noble Muscovite whose attire sufficiently corresponds with that described by Hall in his account of a Russian masque at Westminster, in the reign of Henry VIII., quoted by Ritson in illustration of this play.

"'In the first year of King Henry VIII.,' says the chronicler, 'at a banquet made for the foreign ambassadors in the Parliament-chamber at Westminster, came the Lord Henry Earl of Wiltshire, and the Lord Fitzwalter, in two long gowns of yellow satin traversed with white satin, and in every bend of white was a bend of crimson satin, after the fashion of Russia or Russland, with furred hats of grey on their heads, either of them having an hatchet in their hands, and boots with pikes turned up.' The boots in Vecellio's print have no 'pikes turned up,' but we perceive the 'long gown' of figured satin or damask, and the 'furred hat.' At page 283 of the same work we are presented also with the habit of the Grand Duke of Muscovy, a rich and imposing costume which might be worn by his majesty of Navarre himself." See the cut (copied from K.) on p. 127 above.

122. *Parle.* Parley. Cf. *R. of L.* 100: "parling looks." For the noun, see *Hen. V.* p. 164.

123. *Love-feat.* Plausibly altered by D. and others (Walker's conjecture) to "love-suit;" but *love-feat* may include "the various feats of parleying, courting, and dancing" (Clarke).

125. *Several.* Separate; as often. See *Temp.* p. 131. Cf. the quibble in ii. 1. 222 above.

146. *To the death.* Though death were the consequence of refusal. Cf. *Rich. III.* iii. 2. 55: "I will not do it, to the death."

149. *Speaker's.* From the 1st quarto; "keepers" in the folios.

152. *Ne'er.* The quartos and 1st folio have "ere;" corrected in 2d folio.

159. *Taffeta.* "The taffeta masks they wore to conceal themselves" (Theo.). The early eds. give this line to Biron; corrected by Theo.

160. *Parcel.* For the personal use, cf. *M. of V.* i. 2. 119: "this parcel of wooers;" and *A. W.* ii. 3. 58: "this youthful parcel Of noble bachelors."

166. *Spirits.* Monosyllabic (=*sprites*); as often. Gr. 463.

173. *Brings me out.* Puts me out.

186. *Measure.* A grave and stately dance. Cf. *Much Ado*, ii. 1. 80: "a measure, full of state and ancientry," etc. For *her on this*, the quarto reading, the folios have "you on the."

201. *Accompt.* For the noun, the folio has *accompt* 13 times and *account* 17 times; the verb is always *account* (Schmidt).

207. *Eyne.* An old plural of *eye;* found without the rhyme in *R. of L.* 1229.

209. *Request'st.* The early eds. have "requests." See Gr. 340.

216. *The man.* That is, the man in the moon.

222. *Curtsy.* See on i. 2. 60 above.

233. *Treys.* Threes; as in dice and card playing.

234. *Metheglin.* A sweet beverage. Cf. *M. W.* v. 5. 167 (Evans's speech): "Sack and wine and metheglins." *Wort* is unfermented beer.

236. *Cog.* Deceive; specifically used of falsifying dice.

239. *Change.* Often =exchange, on which sense Maria plays just below.

248. *Veal.* Perhaps punning on the foreign pronunciation of *well* (Malone). Boswell quotes *The Wisdome of Dr. Dodypoll:*

"*Doctor.* Hans, my very speciall friend; fait and trot me be right glad for see you veale.
Hans What, do you make a calfe of me, M. Doctor?"

The Camb. editors say: "The word alluded to is *Viel*, a word which would be likely to be known from the frequent use which the sailors from Hamburg or Bremen would have cause to make of the phrase *zu viel* in their bargains with the London shopkeepers."

260. *The sense of sense.* See on i. 1. 64 above.

264. *Dry-beaten.* Cudgelled, thrashed. See *R. and J.* p. 181, and cf. *C. of E.* p. 119 (note on *Dry basting*).

269. *Well-liking.* Well-conditioned. Cf. what Falstaff says in 1 *Hen. IV.* iii. 3. 6: "I'll repent, while I am in some liking" (while I have some flesh). See also *M. W.* ii. 1. 57. Steevens quotes *Job*, xxix. 4.

270. *Kingly-poor.* Poor for a king; not hyphened in the early eds. and perhaps corrupt. The Coll. MS. has "kill'd by pure," and Sr. reads "wit, stung by poor." St. conjectures "wit, poor-liking."

275. *Weeping-ripe.* Ripe for weeping, ready to weep; used again in 3 *Hen. VI.* i. 4. 172: "What, weeping-ripe, my lord Northumberland?" Cf. *reeling-ripe* in *Temp.* v. 1. 279 and *sinking-ripe* in *C. of E.* i. 1. 78.

278. *No point.* See on ii. 1. 189 above.

280. *Qualm.* Probably a play on *calm*, which seems to have been pronounced like it. Cf. 2 *Hen. IV.* ii. 4. 40 : "sick of a calm ;" and see our ed. p. 167.

282. *Statute-caps.* Woollen caps, which, by act of Parliament in 1571, the citizens were required to wear on Sundays and holidays. The nobility were exempt from the requirement, which, as Strype informs us, was "in behalf of the trade of cappers"—one of sundry such "protection" measures in the time of Elizabeth. The meaning evidently is, that "better wits may be found among citizens" (Steevens), or common folk.

284. *Quick.* Sprightly. See on i. 1. 159 above.

299. *Angels vailing clouds.* That is, letting fall the clouds that have masked or hidden them. For *vail*=lower, let fall, see *M. of V.* p. 128, or *Ham.* p. 179. Theo. reads :

> "Or angel-veiling clouds; are roses blown,
> Dismaskt, their damask sweet commixture shewn ;"

and Warb. the same, except "angels veil'd in " for "angel-veiling."

305. *Shapeless.* Unshapely, ugly ; as in *R. of L.* 973 and *C. of E.* iv. 2. 20.

314. *Thither.* From 1st quarto ; omitted in folios.

317. *As pigeons pease.* Steevens quotes from Ray's *Proverbs :*

> "Children pick up words as pigeons peas,
> And utter them again as God shall please."

318. *God.* The reading of 1st quarto, changed in the folio to "Jove ;" doubtless on account of the statute against the use of the name of God on the stage.

320. *Wassails.* Drinking-bouts, carousals. See *Macb.* p. 180.

325. *Carve.* Carving was considered a courtly accomplishment ; but the word here probably has the same sense as in *M. W.* i. 3. 49 : "She discourses, she carves, she gives the leer of invitation" (see our ed. p. 137), where it refers to making certain signs with the fingers, or a kind of amorous telegraphy.

On *lisp*, cf. *M. W.* iii. 3. 77 : "these lisping hawthorn buds, that come like women in men's apparel," etc.

328. *Tables.* The old name for backgammon.

330. *A mean.* A tenor. Cf. *T. G. of V.* i. 2. 95 : "The mean is drown'd by your unruly base ;" and *W. T.* iv. 3. 46 : "means and bases." Steevens quotes Bacon : "The treble cutteth the air so sharp, as it returneth too swift to make the sound equal ; and therefore a mean or tenor is the sweetest."

334. *Whale's.* A dissyllable. Cf. Spenser, *F. Q.* iii. 1. 15 : "And eke, through feare, as white as whales bone." The simile was a common one in the old poets, as Steevens shows by many quotations. The reference is to the tooth of the walrus, or "horse-whale," then much used as a substitute for ivory.

336. *Boyet.* The rhyme with *debt* is to be noted. Cf. p. 128 above.

340. *This man.* The early eds. have "this madman ;" corrected by Theo. The Camb. ed. retains "madman."

342. *In all hail.* With a play on *hail*=hail-stones (Clarke).

350. *Must break.* Hanmer reads "makes break."

367. *To the manner.* According to the manner, or fashion.

368. *Undeserving praise.* Undeserved praise, or praise to the undeserving. Cf. Gr. 372.

376. *When we greet*, etc. That is, when we look upon the sun it dazzles or blinds our eyes.

391. *We are descried*, etc. This speech and next are spoken aside, as is evident from what the princess says immediately after ; but no former editor, so far as we are aware, has marked them so.

394. *Swoon.* The quartos and 1st folio have "sound," which was one of the ways of spelling the word. It is found in the folio in *M. N. D.* ii. 2. 154, *A. Y. L.* v. 2. 29, *Rich. III.* iv. 1. 35, *R. and J.* iii. 2. 56, etc. The later folios have "swound," which often occurs in the early eds. In *R. of L.* 1486, we find *swounds* rhyming with *wounds*. *Swown* and *swoond* (present) are other old forms.

406. *Friend.* Sometimes =mistress ; as in *M. for M.* i. 4. 29 : "He hath got his friend with child." For the corresponding masculine use, see *Cymb.* p. 171.

409. *Three-pil'd.* Superfine ; or like three-piled velvet, the richest kind. Cf. *M. for M.* i. 2. 33 : "thou art good velvet ; thou 'rt a three-piled piece ;" and *W. T.* iv. 3. 14 : "and in my time wore three-pile."

For *affectation* (Rowe's reading) the early eds. have "affection." See on v. 1. 4 above. W. retains " affection," which he would make a quadrisyllable, rhyming with *ostentati-on*. *Hyperboles*, he says, is a trisyllable, *hy-pér-boles*, as in *T. and C.* i. 3. 161 : "Would seem hyperboles. At this fusty stuff." But *ostentati-on* would make the line an Alexandrine, which (see on i. 1. 108 above) S. rarely used in his early plays ; and it does not seem at all necessary to make *hyperbole* a trisyllable in *T. and C.* *Affectation* is found in the folio in *M. W.* i. 1. 152 and *Ham.* ii. 2. 464 ; *affection* (in the same sense) only here and in v. 1. 4 above.

415. *Russet.* Homespun ; *russet* being a common color for such fabrics. *Kersey* was a coarse woollen stuff.

417. *Sans.* Without ; a French word that had become quite Anglicized in the time of S. See *A. Y. L.* p. 163. In her reply Rosaline bids him speak without *sans*, that is, " without French words " (Tyrwhitt).

421. *Lord have mercy on us.* "The inscription put upon the doors of the houses infected with the plague. The *tokens* of the plague are the first spots or discolorations by which the infection is known to be received" (Johnson). Cf. *A. and C.* iii. 10. 9 : "like the token'd pestilence ;" and see our ed. p. 197.

427. *States.* Estates. See *M. of V.* p. 151, note on *Estate.*

429. *Being those that sue.* A play upon *sue*=prosecute by law (Johnson).

436. *Well-advis'd.* Probably =in your right mind. Cf. *C. of E.* ii. 2. 215 : "mad or well advis'd ?" See also *Rich. III.* p. 192. The ordinary sense of "acting with due deliberation," which most editors give here, seems rather tame.

442. *Force not.* "Make no difficulty" (Johnson), or "care not for"

L

(Schmidt). Cf. *R. of L.* 1021: "I force not argument a straw." Coll. quotes the interlude of *Jacob and Esau*, 1568:

> "O Lorde! some good body, for Gods sake, gyve me meate,
>   I force not what it were, so that I had to eate."

461. *Neither of either.* A common expression of the time, found in *The London Prodigal* and other comedies (Malone).

462. *Consent.* Compact, conspiracy.

465. *Please-man.* Pickthank, parasite.

A *zany* was a subordinate buffoon. Cf. *T. N.* i. 5. 96: "the fools' zanies;" and see our ed. p. 129.

466. *Trencher-knight.* Servingman. Cf. 479 below.

467. *In years.* Probably =into wrinkles, like those of age. Cf. *M. of V.* i. 1. 80: "With mirth and laughter let old wrinkles come." Theo. reads "in jeers."

473. *In will, and error.* "First wilfully, afterwards by mistake" (Clarke).

476. *Squire.* Square, or foot-rule. Cf. *W. T.* p. 199, or 1 *Hen. IV.* p. 159. There is a vulgar proverb, "He has the length of her foot"=he knows her humour exactly (Heath).

477. *Upon the apple of her eye.* In obedience to her glance.

480. *You are allow'd.* "An allowed fool" (*T. N.* i. 5. 101), a privileged jester.

484. *Manage . . . career.* Terms of the stable and the tilt-yard. On *manage*, see *A. Y. L.* p. 136. A *career* was an encounter of knights at full gallop. Cf. *Rich. II.* i. 2. 49, etc. For *manage* the folios have "manager," and the 1st quarto "nuage;" corrected by Theo.

492. *You cannot beg us.* "That is, we are not fools; our next relations cannot *beg* the wardship of our persons and fortunes. One of the legal tests of a *natural* is to try whether he can number" (Johnson). Cf. *C. of E.* p. 116, note on *Fool-begged*. K. remarks: "One of the most abominable corruptions of the feudal system of government was for the sovereign, who was the legal guardian of idiots, to grant the wardship of such an unhappy person to some favourite, granting with the idiot the right of using his property. Ritson, and Douce more correctly, give a curious anecdote illustrative of this custom, and of its abuse:

"'The Lord North begg'd old Bladwell for a foole (though he could never prove him so), and having him in his custodie as a lunaticke, he carried him to a gentleman's house, one day, that was his neighbour. The L. North and the gentleman retir'd awhile to private discourse, and left Bladwell in the dining-roome, which was hung with a faire hanging; Bladwell walking up and downe, and viewing the imagerie, spyed a foole at last in the hanging, and without delay drawes his knife, flyes at the foole, cutts him cleane out, and layes him on the floore; my Lord and the gentleman coming in againe, and finding the tapestrie thus defac'd, he ask'd Bladwell what he meant by such a rude uncivill act; he answered, Sir, be content, I have rather done you a courtesie than a wrong, for, if ever my L. N. had seene the foole there he would have begg'd him, and so you might have lost your whole suite' (*Harl. MS.* 6395)."

502. *Whereuntil.* Whereunto, to what.

503. *Pursent.* The early eds. have "parfect" or "perfect" (corrected by W.), and "in" for *e'en* (corrected by Malone).

504. *Pompion.* The early eds. have here "Pompey;" corrected by Rowe.

517, 518. *Where zeal,* etc. We leave this passage as in the folio (with W. and the Camb. editors), in preference to adopting any one of the many emendations that have been proposed. The plural *contents* is used for the sake of the rhyme; and the meaning seems to be: where zeal strives to please, but the very effort is fatal to the pleasure. The context is the best commentary upon it. For the singular *Dies,* see Gr. 333.

Hanmer reads "content Dies in the zeal of that it doth present;" Steevens, "contents Die in the zeal of them which it presents;" Sr. and H., "contents Lie in the fail of that which it presents;" and Clarke (Mason's conjecture), "content Lies in the zeal of those which it present." For other conjectures, see the Camb. ed.

527. *Honey.* For the personal use, cf. 1 *Hen. IV.* i. 2. 179, *T. and C.* v. 2. 18, *R. and J.* ii. 5. 18, etc.

529. *Fortuna de la guerra.* Fortune of war (Spanish). Hanmer has "della guerra," forgetting that Armado is a Spaniard and not an Italian. The early eds. have "delaguar;" and Schmidt conjectures "del agua" (of the water, alluding to the old saying that swimming must be tried in the water) or "de la guarda" (of guard, "that is, guarding Fortune").

531. *Couplement.* Used here for *couple.* In *Sonn.* 21. 5 it is =combination.

542. *Novum.* Hanmer reads "novem." *Novum* (or *novem*) was a game at dice. Steevens quotes Greene, *Art of Legerdemain,* 1612: "The principal use of them [dice] is at novum," etc. *Abate* =leave out, except; and the meaning is: "except in a throw at novum, the whole world could not furnish five such."

543. *Pick.* The reading of 1st quarto; the other early eds. have "prick."

546. *Libbard's.* Leopard's; the knee-caps in old dresses and plate-armour often being in the form of a leopard's head (D.).

563. *Stands too right.* According to Plutarch, Alexander's head had a twist towards the left. The next line alludes to the statement of the same author that Alexander's skin had "a marvellous good savour."

572. *The painted cloth.* For the historical and other paintings on the cloth hangings of rooms, see *A. Y. L.* p. 176.

573. *That holds his poll-axe,* etc. The arms of Alexander, as given in the old history of the Nine Worthies, were a lion sitting in a chair holding a battle-axe (Tollet).

574. *Ajax.* There is a play on *a jakes;* a coarse joke that occurs in B. J., Camden, Sir John Harington, and other writers of the time.

575. *Afeard.* The quarto has *afeard,* and the folios *afraid.* The forms are used interchangeably in the early eds.

580. *A little o'erparted.* With a *part,* or *rôle,* a little too much for him.

582. *Stand aside,* etc. The Coll. MS. here has the stage direction "*Exit Costard;*" not noted in the Camb. ed. W. (apparently misled

by Coll.) ascribes this stage-direction to the folio. See on 657 and 662 below.

583. *Imp.* Youngster. See on i. 2. 5 above.

584. *Canus.* Dog (Latin *canis*); reading of the early eds., which may be retained for the sake of the rhyme. Rowe reads "canis."

593. *Ycliped.* Yclept; mispronounced for the sake of the joke that follows.

605. *A cittern-head.* A *cittern* (cithern, gittern, or guitar) often had a grotesque face carved upon its *head.*

610. *Flask.* That is, a powder-flask; as in *R. and J.* iii. 3. 132.

611. *Half-cheek in a brooch.* Profile on a clasp, or buckle. Cf. *half-face* in *K. John,* i. 1. 92.

625. *Baited.* Worried; like a *baited* bear or bull.

628. *Come home by me.* That is, come home to me.

630. *Trojan.* The early eds. have "Troyan," as often elsewhere. The word was much used as a term of contempt. See 1 *Hen. IV.* p. 158.

635. *The small.* That is, of the leg.

638. *Lances.* Lancers; as in *Lear,* v. 3. 50: "our impress'd lances," etc.

640. *A gilt nutmeg.* Mentioned by B. J. in his *Christmas Masque* as a present (Steevens). The 1st quarto has "gift" for *gilt.* An orange or lemon, *stuck with cloves,* was a common new-year's gift.

647. *Breath'd.* Endowed with breath, or "wind." Cf. *A. and C.* iii. 13. 178: "treble-sinew'd, hearted, breath'd."
For *fight ye* (Rowe's reading) the early eds. have "fight; yea."

655, 656. *When he breathed . . . man.* From the 1st quarto; not in the folios.

657. After this line Capell gives the stage-direction, "*Biron steps to Costard and whispers him;*" that is, putting him up to the trick on Armado.

662. *This Hector,* etc. After this speech Coll. gives, from his MS., the stage-direction "*Re-enter Costard, in haste, unarmed;*" not noted in the Camb. ed. Coll. remarks: "Unless he had gone out, it is not easy to see how he had obtained the information he brings." D., who adopts Capell's stage-direction at 657 just above, has here "*Costard [suddenly coming from behind].* The party is gone," etc. W., who makes Costard leave at 582 above, has at 657 "*Birone goes out,*" and here "*Enter* Costard *hastily and unarmed, and* Birone *after him.*" It is doubtful just how the trick was meant to be managed, and any one of the ways suggested by the editors would do well enough on the stage. It could safely be left to the actors without any stage-direction, as in the Camb. ed.

663. *The party is gone.* Printed in italics as a stage-direction in the early eds.

671. *Quick by him.* There is a play on *quick*=alive. See *Hen. V.* p. 156, and cf. *Acts,* x. 42, etc.

678. *More Ates.* "That is, more instigation. *Ate* was the mischievous goddess that incited bloodshed" (Johnson). Cf. *Much Ado,* p. 132.

684. *Fight with a pole,* etc. That is, with the quarter-staff, a long pole, in the use of which the men of the North of England were skilful.

685. *I pray you.* The 1st quarto has "bepray."

686. *My arms.* "The weapons and armour which he wore in his character of Pompey" (Johnson).

690. *Let me take you,* etc. "Perhaps =let me speak without ceremony" (Schmidt).

700. *Woolward.* That is, with woollen next to the skin, or without linen. Grey quotes Stowe's *Annals:* "he went woolward and barefooted to many churches, in every of them to pray to God for help in his blindness." Farmer adds from Lodge's *Incarnate Devils,* 1596: "His common course is to go always untrust [untrussed]; except when his shirt is a washing, and then he goes woolward."

713. *I have seen,* etc. "Armado means to say in his affected style, that he had discovered that he was wronged, and was determined to right himself as a soldier" (Mason). "One may see day at a little hole" is found in Ray's *Proverbs. Through the little hole of discretion* may be ="though discreetly forbearing from righting myself until I can do it with dignity," as Steevens and Clarke explain it.

723. *Liberal.* Too free, over-bold. It is used in a yet stronger sense in *Much Ado,* iv. 1. 93: "a liberal villain," etc. See our ed. p. 154, or *Ham.* p. 258.

725. *Converse of breath.* That is, in conversation. For the accent of *converse,* cf. *Oth.* iii. 1. 40. Steevens compares *M. of V.* v. 1. 141: "this breathing courtesy" (that is, these courteous words).

727. *Nimble.* The early eds. have "humble;" corrected by Theo. The Coll. MS. changes *not* to "but."

730. *The extreme parts of time,* etc. We retain the folio reading, which Dr. B. Nicholson (*Trans. of New. Shaks. Soc.* for 1874, p. 513) explains thus: "The *extreme parts* are the end parts, *extremities*—as, of our body, the fingers; of chains, the final links; of given portions of time, the last of those units into which we choose to divide them. Afterwards (in 777) the King, representing the stay of the Princess as for an hour, calls *the extreme part* 'the latest minute,' and the thought in both passages is so far the same. It is not however said that our decision is necessitated by the extremity of the moment, though this is perhaps suggested to us by the sound of the words used; but that concurring circumstances, and therefore *Time,* as the producer of those circumstances, so influence our decision that he, and not we, may be called the decider. Hence Time, as personified, and as the intelligential agent of whom the extreme parts are but the instrumental members, is considered as the true nominative to the verb *forms,* and is represented as fashioning or moulding all causes or questions to the purposes of his speed, that is, to his own intents, or to those of the fate or Providence of which he is the sub-agent. This thought has been forced upon the King by finding that his high resolves of study were at once broken by the coming of the Princess, while her sudden departure shows him that he cannot do without her love; and he urges it as an excuse for the intrusion of his love on her time of grief, and as an excuse for her favourable reply.

"In the next lines, though still personifying Time, the King changes his illustration. Often the archer may weigh variously all the circumstances

—the bow, the arrow, the intended strength of shot and elevation, the wind and the like—and so vary from moment to moment; but *at the very loose*, or loosing of the shaft (an act the proper doing of which was much dwelt on by archers) he comes to a quick and determined decision. 'So during your stay, princess,' says the King, 'I and my lords acted doubtfully between our former resolves and our new loves, and you have dallied with us: now at your departure, at the last moment, I decide and ask your love; do you answer with the same determinateness.' In retort, the Princess most consistently decides in accord with the events which Time has purposed in her regard, for the declaration of the King is only one of these, another and the first being the news of her father's death.

"The thought of the first two lines is allied and similar to Hamlet's

> 'There's a divinity that shapes our ends,
> Rough-hew them as we will;'

just as the rest expresses the similar idea specially illustrated in the catastrophe of that play. But here the subject being of a gentler nature, the King speaks more conversationally and less reflectively than Hamlet does, and of *Time* and not of a Providence or *divinity*."

D. reads "part" for *parts*, Sr. and W. "haste," and St. and H. "dart." It is plausibly urged in support of the last that it is in keeping with the figure in *loose ;* but it is common enough for a figure to be introduced in the course of a passage, and here it is naturally suggested by the reference to the *speed* with which time flies. *Forms* has been changed to "form," but quite unnecessarily. Cf. Gr. 333.

Extreme is accented on the first syllable because preceding the noun. See on *profound*, in iv. 3. 163 above.

736. *Convince.* Overcome, conquer. See *Macb.* pp. 180, 242.

742. *Dull.* The early eds. have "double." *Dull* is from the Coll. MS. and is adopted by W. and H. Capell reads "deaf," and St. conjectures "hear dully."

750. *Strains.* Impulses, vagaries. Cf. *M. W.* ii. 1. 91, *T. of A.* iv. 3. 213, etc.

751. *Skipping.* Flighty, frivolous. Cf. *M. of V.* ii. 2. 196:

> "Pray thee, take pain
> To allay with some cold drops of modesty
> Thy skipping spirit, lest through thy wild behaviour
> I be misconstrued," etc.

753. *Strange.* The early eds. have "straying;" corrected by Capell. Coleridge conjectured "stray."

758. *Have misbecom'd.* Capell changed *Have* to "'T hath;" but the "confusion of construction" is like many other instances in S. Cf. Gr. 411–416 (in 418 Abbott compares this passage with a Latin idiom, but the coincidence is doubtless accidental).

For the form *misbecom'd*, cf. *becomed* in *R. and J.* iv. 2. 26, *A. and C.* iii. 7. 26, and *Cymb.* v. 5. 406.

760. *Suggested.* Tempted; as in *Oth.* ii. 3. 358:

> " When devils will the blackest sins put on,
> They do suggest at first with heavenly shows."

See also *Rich. II.* pp. 153, 198. Cf. *suggestions* in i. 1. 156 above.

771. *Bombast.* Originally, *cotton* used to stuff out garments. Cf. the quotation from Stubbes in note on iii. 1. 15 above. Gerarde, in his *Herbal*, calls the cotton plant "the bombast tree;" and Lupton, in *A Thousand Notable Things*, speaks of a candle "with a wick of bumbast."

772. *This in our.* The 1st quarto has "this our," and the folios "these are our;" corrected by Hanmer. *Respects* = considerations, thoughts.

776. *Quote.* Construe, interpret. Cf. *misquote* = misconstrue, in 1 *Hen. IV.* v. 2. 13, the only instance of the word in S. See also ii. 1. 245 above.

779. *World-without-end.* Cf. *Sonn.* 57. 5 :

> " Nor dare I chide the world-without-end hour
> Whilst I, my sovereign, watch the clock for you."

781. *Dear.* Used in an intensive sense ; as in 854 below. See also on ii. 1. 1 above.

791. *Weeds.* Garments. See *M. N. D.* p. 149.

793. *Last love.* "Continue to be love" (Steevens).

795. *Challenge me, challenge me.* Hanmer omits the first *me ;* not noted in the Camb. ed.

804. *Flatter up.* Hanmer reads "fetter up." For the *up*, see on iv. 3. 300 above. The meaning is : "in order that I might soothe or pamper these faculties of mine by leading a life of repose" (Clarke).

807-812. *And what . . . sick.* Enclosed in brackets by Theo. and omitted by Hanmer. It is evidently a part of the first sketch which was rewritten in revising the play. See on iv. 3. 294 above.

808. *Rank.* The early eds. have "rack'd ;" corrected by Rowe. Cf. *Ham.* iii. 3. 36 : "O, my offence is rank," etc.

809. *Attaint.* Attainted. For the form, see Gr. 342.

814. *A wife?* The early eds. give this to Katherine, reading : "A wife? a beard, faire health," etc. Hanmer has "No wife : a beard," etc. D. was the first to transfer *A wife?* to Dumain, in whose mouth it seems more natural.

835. *All estates.* All kinds or conditions of people ; as in *Rich. III.* iii. 7. 213 : "And equally, indeed, to all estates." Latimer, in his *Sermons*, says it is the duty of a king "to see to all estates, to provide for the poor," etc. For *execute* the Coll. MS. has "exercise."

843. *Fierce.* Ardent, strenuous ; as in *Lear*, ii. 1. 36, etc.

854. *Dear.* Changed by the Coll. MS. to "dire." See on 781 above.

855. *Continue them.* The early eds. have "then ;" corrected in the Coll. MS.

859. *Reformation.* Metrically five syllables. Gr. 479.

863. *Bring you.* Accompany you. Cf. *W. T.* iv. 3. 122 : "Shall I bring thee on the way?" See also *Gen.* xviii. 16, *Acts*, xxi. 5, 2 *Cor.* i. 16, etc.

865. *Jack hath not Jill.* Cf. *M. N. D.* iii. 2. 461 : "Jack shall have Jill ;" and see our ed. p. 171.

882. *Pied.* Variegated. Cf. *M. of V.* i. 3. 80 : "streak'd and pied," etc.

883, 884. *And lady-smocks*, etc. These two lines are transposed in all the early eds.; corrected by Theo.

Lady-smocks. Ellacombe (*Plant-Lore of S.*) says : "*Lady-smocks* are the flowers of Cardamine pratensis, the pretty early meadow flower of which children are so fond, and of which the popularity is shown by its many names, Lady-smocks, Cuckoo-flower, Meadow Cress, Pinks, Spinks, Bog-spinks, and May-flower, and 'in Northfolke, Canterbury Bells.' The origin of the name is not very clear. It is generally explained from the resemblance of the flowers to smocks hung out to dry, but the resemblance seems to me rather far-fetched. According to another explanation, 'the Lady-smock, a corruption of Our Lady's-smock, is so called from its first flowering about Lady-tide. It is a pretty purplish-white, tetradynamous plant, which blows from Lady-tide till the end of May, and which during the latter end of April covers the moist meadows with its silvery-white, which looks at a distance like a white sheet spread over the fields' (*Circle of the Seasons*). Those who adopt this view called the plant Our Lady's-smock, but I cannot find that name in any old writers. Drayton, coeval with Shakespeare, says :

> 'Some to grace the show,
> Of Lady-smocks most white do rob each neighbouring mead,
> Wherewith their loose locks most curiously they braid.'

And Isaac Walton, in the next century, drew that pleasant picture of himself sitting quietly by the waterside—'looking down the meadows I could see here a boy gathering Lilies and Lady-smocks, and there a girl cropping Culverkeys and Cowslips.'"

884. *Cuckoo-buds.* "There is a difficulty in deciding what flower Shakespeare meant by Cuckoo-buds. We now always give the name to the Meadow Cress (Cardamine pratensis), but it cannot be that in either of these passages, because that flower is mentioned under its other name of Lady-smocks in the previous line, nor is it 'of yellow hue ;' nor does it grow among Corn, as described in *Lear*, iv. 4. 4. Many plants have been suggested, but I think the Buttercup, as suggested by Dr. Prior, will best meet the requirements" (Ellacombe). Farmer conjectures "cowslip-buds," and Whalley "crocus-buds."

887. *Mocks married men.* The note of the *cuckoo* was thought to prognosticate cuckoldom. Cf. *M. N. D.* iii. 1. 134 and *A. W.* i. 3. 67. See also *M. W.* p. 143.

893. *Turtles.* Turtle-doves. See on iv. 3. 207 above.

900. *Hang by the wall.* That is, from the eaves. Malone compares *Hen. V.* iii. 5. 23 and *Temp.* v. 1. 17.

901. *Blows his nail.* To warm his fingers. Cf. *3 Hen. VI.* ii. 5. 3 : "the shepherd, blowing of his nails." See also *T. of S.* i. 1. 109.

906, 907. *Tu-whoo*, etc. The early eds. have only "Tu-whit to-who," both here and in the next stanza. Capell was the first to make the measure correspond with that of the preceding stanzas.

908. *Keel.* Cool ; that is, by stirring it. Clarke says the word came also to mean skimming off the scum that rose to the top, which may be the sense here. Coll. quotes *Piers Plowman:*

> "And lerede men a ladel bygge, with a long stele
> That caste for to kele a crockke, and save the fatte above;"

that is, they skimmed the crock, or pot, with a ladle, in order to save the fat. Schmidt also defines *keel* as "to scum (German *kielen*)."

910. *Saw.* Moral saying, maxim. Cf. *A. Y. L.* ii. 7. 156: "Full of wise saws;" 2 *Hen. VI.* i. 3. 61: "holy saws of sacred writ," etc.

913. *Crabs.* Crab-apples; often roasted and put into the wassail-bowl. Cf. *M. N. D.* ii. 1. 48 (Puck's speech):

> "And sometime lurk I in a gossip's bowl,
> In very likeness of a roasted crab;

and see our ed. p. 140.

ADDENDUM.

THE "TIME-ANALYSIS" OF THE PLAY.—This is given by Mr. P. A. Daniel, in his paper "On the Times or Durations of the Action of Shakspere's Plays" (*Trans. of New Shaks. Soc.* 1877-79, p. 145) as follows:

"*Day* 1.—The first day of the action includes Acts I. and II. In it the Princess of France has her first interview with the King of Navarre. Toward the end of Act II. certain documents required for the establishment of the French claims are stated to have not yet come; but, says Boyet, '*to-morrow* you shall have a sight of them' (l. 165), and the King tells the Princess—'*To-morrow* shall we visit you again' (l. 176).

"*Day* 2.—Act III. Armado intrusts Costard with a letter to Jaquenetta; immediately afterwards Biron also intrusts him with a letter for Rosaline, which he is to deliver *this afternoon* (l. 153).

"Act IV. sc. i. The Princess remarks that '*to-day* we shall have our dispatch.' This fixes the scene as the *morrow* referred to in the first day. Costard now enters to deliver, as he supposes, the letter intrusted to him by Biron. He mistakes, however, and gives up Armado's letter to Jaquenetta.

"Act IV. sc. ii. Costard and Jaquenetta come to Holofernes and Nathaniel to get them to read the letter, as they suppose, of Armado to Jaquenetta. It turns out to be the letter of Biron to Rosaline, and Costard and Jaquenetta are sent off to give it up at once to the King. It is clear that these scenes from the beginning of Act III. are all on one day; but at the end of this scene Holofernes invites Nathaniel and Dull to *dine* with him 'to day at the father's of a pupil of mine.' This does not agree very well with 'this afternoon' mentioned in Act III., and one or the other—the *afternoon*, I think—must be set down as an oversight.

"Act IV. sc. iii. Still the same day. The King, Longaville, and Dumain mutually detect each other of love, and Biron triumphs over all three till his own backslidings are exposed by the entry of Costard and Jaquenetta with his letter to Rosaline. Finally, all four resolve to woo their mistresses openly, and determine that—

> '———in the *afternoon*
> [They] will with some strange pastime solace them' (l. 371, 372).

"In pursuance of this idea in the next scene, Act V. sc. i., we find Armado consulting Holofernes and Nathaniel — who have now returned from their dinner—as to some masque with which 'it is the King's most sweet pleasure and affection to congratulate the Princess at her pavilion in the posteriors of this day, which the rude multitude call the afternoon' (l. 77–80). A masque of the Nine Worthies is determined on.

"In the next scene the masque is presented accordingly, and with this scene the Play ends.

"The time of the action, then, is two days:

"1. Acts I. and II.

"2. Acts III. to V."

INDEX OF WORDS AND PHRASES EXPLAINED.

INTERIOR OF ANNE HATHAWAY'S COTTAGE.

SHAKESPEARE.

WITH NOTES BY WM. J. ROLFE, A.M.

ILLUSTRATED. 16MO, CLOTH, 56 CTS. PER VOL.; PAPER, 40 CTS. PER VOL.

In the preparation of this edition of the English Classics it has been the aim to adapt them for school and home reading, in essentially the same way as Greek and Latin Classics are edited for educational purposes. The chief requisites are a pure text (expurgated, if necessary), and the notes needed for its thorough explanation and illustration.

Each of Shakespeare's plays is complete in one volume, and is preceded by an Introduction containing the "History of the Play," the "Sources of the Plot," and "Critical Comments on the Play."

From HORACE HOWARD FURNESS, Ph.D., LL.D., *Editor of the "New Variorum Shakespeare."*

No one can examine these volumes and fail to be impressed with the conscientious accuracy and scholarly completeness with which they are edited. The educational purposes for which the notes are written Mr. Rolfe never loses sight of, but like "a well-experienced archer hits the mark his eye doth level at."

From F. J. FURNIVALL, *Director of the New Shakspere Society, London.*

The merit I see in Mr. Rolfe's school editions of Shakspere's Plays over those most widely used in England is that Mr. Rolfe edits the plays as works of a poet, and not only as productions in Tudor English. Some editors think that all they have to do with a play is to state its source and explain its hard words and allusions ; they treat it as they would a charter or a catalogue of household furniture, and then rest satisfied. But Mr. Rolfe, while clearing up all verbal difficulties as carefully as any Dryasdust, always adds the choicest extracts he can find, on the spirit and special "note" of each play, and on the leading characteristics of its chief personages. He does *not* leave the student without help in getting at Shakspere's chief attributes, his characterization and poetic power. And every practical teacher knows that while every boy can look out hard words in a lexicon for himself, not one in a score can, unhelped, catch points of and realize character, and feel and express the distinctive individuality of each play as a poetic creation.

From Prof. EDWARD DOWDEN, LL.D., *of the University of Dublin,*
Author of "Shakspere: His Mind and Art."

I incline to think that no edition is likely to be so useful for school and home reading as yours. Your notes contain so much accurate instruction, with so little that is superfluous ; you do not neglect the æsthetic study of the play ; and in externals, paper, type, binding, etc., you make a book "pleasant to the eyes" (as well as "to be desired to make one wise ")—no small matter, I think, with young readers and with old.

From EDWIN A. ABBOTT, M.A., *Author of "Shakespearian Grammar."*

I have not seen any edition that compresses so much necessary information into so small a space, nor any that so completely avoids the common faults of commentaries on Shakespeare—needless repetition, superfluous explanation, and unscholar-like ignoring of difficulties.

From HIRAM CORSON, M.A., *Professor of Anglo-Saxon and English*
Literature, Cornell University, Ithaca, N. Y.

In the way of annotated editions of separate plays of Shakespeare, for educational purposes, I know of none quite up to Rolfe's.